Éclairs and Executions:
Alphabet Soup Mysteries

Book 5

Erica J Whelton

Publisher: Sunseri Design Publishing
Cover Designer: Mariah Sinclair Book Cover Design
ISBN: 978-1-956069-32-7

Printed in the United States of America

Dedicated to found family!

Chapter One

"You have everything for school?" I asked as we pulled into the parking lot at the J.W. Dashwood Fine Arts High School.

"Yes, thanks, mom." Shayla laughed.

She wasn't my daughter, but one of my employees. Recently, she moved in with me and my roommates, because a few weeks ago, her stepfather beat her, sending her to the hospital.

Plus, she had an explosive relationship with her mother, Kenna. After Shayla was discharged from the hospital, Kenna washed her hands of her oldest daughter.

So, long story short, Shayla has been living with me ever since.

Somehow, over these past few weeks, I have slipped into a motherly role. A job I never thought I'd have, but here I am with a nearly eighteen-year-old.

"And do you need a ride to your parents' house this afternoon?"

"No, I will take the bus and then order a ride share home."

"You sure? I bet Hannah would cover for me, so I could take off an hour early."

It was just an hour, and it was during our slow time, so I could easily get away.

"I'll let you know, but for now, my plan is bus and then ride share." She smiled. "Have a great day."

"You, too."

I watched her hop out. She jogged over to a few friends, greeting and laughing with them. This made me so happy. I hadn't seen her with friends, just getting to be a teenager.

When I first met her roughly five months ago, she was a serious, quiet girl, walking around as if she had the weight of the world on her shoulders. She opened up a bit while at the restaurant, talking and joking with the other staff, but still kept herself guarded.

Still, it was good to see her for just a moment, being a kid.

But the biggest transformation had come in the past few weeks, since being away from her family. The weight of responsibility and abuse had been lifted. She could simply be a high school student enjoying her last few months of high school.

I headed across town to the restaurant. I would be a little early, but it didn't matter. I loved being at the restaurant when it was empty. It got my creative juices going. Maybe I could brainstorm a new dish or perfect a current one.

A few hours later, we opened, and we had a special for the day ready to go. It was a honey Dijon roasted chicken with rice pilaf and steamed broccoli. When Noah came in, I asked him to post it on our website and the various social media sites.

"That should get us some buzz, right?" I asked him.

"Heck, yeah! That was a brilliant idea Cullen had. I can't believe I didn't think of it."

I assigned my newest line cook, Eli, to Hannah's station and had staged a new setup for Hannah. Since she's my most experienced cook, I thought she was ready to take on more responsibilities and become a sous chef and, at times, take over as the executive chef when I was out.

I loved my job and had no intention of stepping back at least too much, but it would be nice to go on vacation or hit the competition circuit again. I missed the rush and adrenaline of the on-the-fly recipes from mystery ingredients, meeting new chefs, and, of course, the times I won were the best.

I have been to many major cities and seen lots of sights. Now that she's retired, it would be fun to take Auntie Rita with me. She and Granny Ines had gone on a few trips with me, but at the time, they both had to work.

Plus, I had June and Parker in the evenings. Now it would be me and Hannah as the executive chef for the day shift.

My alphabet soup was created for one of these competitions from when I was in high school at the culinary arts school. Shayla would soon be getting ready for a similar competition through the school. My pastry chef, Natalie was mentoring her as she prepared for the competition in the pastry and baking category.

They were working on éclairs. It was an excellent idea. Simple concept, yet the skies the limit on combinations of flavors. The competition was in December, just before Shayla graduated. It would be her final project.

She had a full-time job here once she graduated, but I supported her if she decided to go on to college or if she wanted to work at a different restaurant. Though, selfishly, I wanted her to pick my restaurant.

Skye called out that she was going to unlock the front door for the day.

"Here we go Crock Potters! Time for another wonderful day."

"Game faces." Ripley laughed.

"Love the energy," Noah yelled as he moved from the kitchen to the dining room.

Within a few minutes, our first orders came in and they didn't stop coming for a few hours.

"It's Monday. Why were we so busy today?" Hannah said with a laugh. "We were slammed."

"I have no idea, but how many of those specials do you think you made?"

"I couldn't even guess. A few dozen easily."

"I guess I need to come up with a few more specials," I mused.

"Yes, you do."

"And Cullen is brilliant for his advertising strategy."

She nodded as she got to work cleaning and stocking her station again.

I did the same, then I walked around, touching base with the various kitchen staff to see if they needed anything or had any feedback. Once I'd talked to everyone, I went to the office to see if Noah was there.

He must still be out front.

I checked my phone. There was a missed call and a few text messages. One of the messages was from Shayla letting me know she had a ride home. Then the missed call and remaining message were from my friend, Officer Kyle Rafferty.

R: **I need you to come to the station asap!**

My heart slammed to a stop. What was wrong? Was it Granny, Auntie Rita, or one of my roommates-slash-best friends, Sawyer and Vee?

I hit his number to return his call.

"Jess, thank you for calling. Are you able to come into the station?" Rafferty asked. He didn't even say hello, just got right to business, which had me in a near panic.

"Yes, what's wrong? Who's in trouble?"

He let out a breath. "It's Shayla. She's okay, but her stepfather and mother have been killed. She was standing over the bodies when officers arrived."

"What? Ohmygosh, yes, yes, I am on my way." I hung up, grabbing my purse. As I whirled around to rush out of the office, I almost slammed right into Noah.

"Whoa, Chef, what's wrong?"

"Shayla's stepfather and mother were found dead. They have her at the station."

"Do you want me to drive you?"

"We can't both leave," I said, even though it would be nice to have him along.

"Darn, you're right." Noah frowned. "Let me know what you learn."

"I will."

I stopped on my way out to make sure Hannah would be able to take over my station for the rest of my shift.

"Of course, Chef. Go help Shayla," she said, tears in her eyes. "That poor girl."

"She has had a rough life." I bit my tongue to prevent saying more because a lot of us have, but right now, this was about Shayla. "Thanks for your help."

Opening the back door, I found that it was raining. I groaned as I ran to my car.

"Great," I said when I got into my car.

I grabbed a few tissues from my center console, wiping my face as best I could. Checking myself in the mirror, I looked like a mess. Oh, well. I was going to save my employee.

I shot off a text message to my roommates, Vee and Sawyer. They would want to know since they have both gotten to think of her as our fourth roommate and a little sister. We all did.

Their replies came after I was driving. The car read them for me.

V: **Oh, that poor girl. Do you need us?**

S: **We can meet you there.**

My car asked if I wanted to reply. I thought about what I wanted to say. Finally, I did reply.

Me: **No, let me see what is going on and I'll let you know.**

With that, I continued to the police station. A mix of emotions ran through me, and the ride over felt like I would never get there.

My mind raced through scenario after scenario, but until I got there, I wouldn't know for sure what was happening or how she was doing.

Chapter Two

I arrived at the police station and parked in a visitor's spot. I hesitated, not wanting to face this, but I knew Shayla had no one else. Plus, I had promised her I had her back.

Taking a few deep breaths, I headed in.

Officer Dorian was at the reception desk. I had only met him twice, but his blank stare had me thinking he didn't recognize me. Not that I expected him to, but since I had been called to come in, I thought he would at least be expecting me.

"Hello. Can I help you?"

"Yes, Officer Rafferty asked me to come in."

"Have a seat. I'll give him a call." He grabbed the desk phone, but before he could dial, the door behind him opened, and Rafferty walked out.

"Jess, good, you're here." He gestured to me to follow him, his usually smiling face creased with worry.

I nodded and followed him as he led the way through the bullpen of the station. There were a lot of officers in the office at the moment. They fell silent when they saw me.

Officers Roberts and Perez nodded hello. Chief Stone looked at me, rolled his eyes, then slammed the door to his office.

Well, that was rude. We had had an interesting history, so it honestly wasn't that surprising.

Raff stopped at a conference room, gesturing for me to enter. I looked around, taking a seat where he pointed. When I didn't see Shayla, my heart sped up. Where was she?

I flipped around to ask him. He smiled softly, putting a hand on my arm.

"I want to fill you in about what is going on before I get Shayla."

He was a mind reader.

"Alright, but is she okay?"

"Yeah, she's okay. Upset, obviously, but safe and in the next room."

I stood, but then knew I needed to hear the details, so I sat again. I flashed him a weak smile.

"Sorry, what happened?"

"Her stepfather and mother were found shot. The stepfather was deceased when we arrived, but her mother was still hanging on. Shayla was there, covered in blood." His eyes met mine.

"Wait, are you saying she's a suspect?" I sat forward.

He frowned. "No, no. Well, yes."

"What?" I blurted.

"Now wait, let me explain. I don't think she would do this, but it looks bad."

"Where is Detective Upton?"

"He's still at the scene. They are gathering forensics and talking to neighbors and witnesses."

"There are witnesses?"

He shook his head. "Some neighbors heard the shots, but we haven't found anyone who saw anything. It happened inside the house."

"Okay, but why do you say it looks bad for Shayla? What makes her a suspect?"

"She was holding the gun in one hand and her mother in the other when we arrived."

"What? There's no way."

No, that doesn't sound good, but I knew she wasn't the shooter. I had to admit, though, it didn't look good for her, and I could see why the police immediately thought she did it.

If it was just her holding her mother, that's one thing. I did the same when my sous chef, Earl, was killed on the night we opened the restaurant. I could still see him in my mind. His blank eyes. The hole in his chest. All the blood.

No matter how this turned out, that part will haunt her forever.

"Wait! If she did it, how did you get there so fast that she would still have been holding the gun?"

"Um, that … I don't know. A neighbor called and said that they heard a shot. We arrived roughly six minutes later. The front door was open, and I could hear her crying out. That's when I found her."

"You're the one?"

"Yes. Roberts and I were first on the scene, but I was the first in the house."

"And why are you telling me all of this?"

"Because you're her guardian, at least since the incident with her stepfather and her mother signed those papers to allow her to live with you."

"Oh, she actually signed them. I didn't know."

"Nobody told you? She signed them last week." He held up a finger, signaling he needed a minute. He left the room, coming back a moment later with papers. "Here. That's a copy for you."

I read them. Yes, in fact, here it was. Kenna Stokes had signed over a power of attorney to me.

"I didn't know that she had officially done this." I looked at it once more. "Now what?"

"Now, do you want to see her?"

"Of course." I popped up and followed him to the next room.

Walking in, my heart sunk. There she was, looking so small and helpless, still in her blood-soaked clothes. She was quietly sobbing. She slowly looked up. When our eyes locked, a small, choking sound came from deep inside her. My heart instantly broke.

"Jess?" Her voice catching in her throat.

I went to her immediately, wrapping my arms around her.

"It's okay. It's okay. I'm so sorry," I whispered as she began crying heavily.

We stayed like that for a few minutes while Raff just stood at the doorway looking around awkwardly.

"Can we get her some clean clothes? Is she allowed to wash up a little bit, too?" I asked.

"Oh, yeah, of course. Let me … um, let me figure it out." He looked her up and down. "You're a small?"

She looked at me, then back at him, nodding. He bobbed his head once and left. With him gone, I took advantage of being alone with her.

"Are you okay?"

"My mother … she died in my arms."

"I'm so sorry." I squeezed her hand. "What happened?"

"I took the bus home so I could get my stuff, figuring I would get a ride share back to your place, our place. When I arrived, I went in the front door. Nobody was there, but I heard the back door slam shut. Since I didn't see anyone, I went to my room. Then I heard a weird sound from down the hall, from my mom's room. I went to see what was going on. That's when I saw her and Mikey on the floor. He was clearly dead, but mom was still breathing. It was shallow. She reached for me."

Shayla's voice wavered, but she took a couple of deep breaths. "Her voice was so quiet. She said *They will get me, too.* I asked who, and she tried to say a name, but I couldn't make out what she was saying. That's when I saw the gun. I picked it up. Gawd, I don't even know what I was thinking."

She wiped her eyes as new tears fell. Blood smeared across her face as she wiped it with her sweatshirt sleeve.

"And that's when the police arrived?"

"Yes. She took her last breath in my arms just as Officer Rafferty came in." She fell against me, crying again.

That's when Officer Perez came in holding a bag. She looked at me and then at Shayla, giving us a half-smile.

"I brought clothes and can escort you to the bathroom. Our bathroom, not the public one. We have showers in there."

Shayla stood, looking down at me. It looked as though she wanted to say something.

"Do you want me to come with you?" I asked.

"Yes, wait. No, I can go by myself." She straightened her back, holding her head high, but she didn't move.

I could understand her desire to be independent and confident, but I could see the wide-eyed little girl deep inside. She was scared and there were many reasons to feel that way. She was now an orphan at only seventeen and a suspect in murder.

There was no reason for her to do this by herself when I was here and knew many of her feelings.

"You don't have to do this all alone. You aren't alone."

She looked at Officer Perez. "Can she come with me?"

"Of course."

"Great." I stood, wrapping an arm around her shoulders, then together we followed Officer Perez.

We entered the bathroom and locker room area. It was quiet here away from the noisy bullpen area. There were two bathroom stalls, two sinks, and a row of a dozen dark green lockers. Only one had a lock on it.

"I'm the only female currently, at least since Wilson left last year, so this should be private for you." She smiled. "There are showers back that way, and I put some shampoo and soap in that bag. You can find a towel hanging by the shower."

"Thank you," Shayla mumbled.

"I'll wait out here, but holler if you need anything," I said as I sat on the wooden bench. She nodded and disappeared into the other room. Lupe Perez took a seat on the other side of the bench.

"You think she did it?" Perez asked me.

"No, there's no way. She's the sweetest girl. Funny and generous."

"Yeah, I agree. She's been dealt a bad hand in life." She mumbled, looking over her shoulder, "there is a theory about it being a murder-suicide."

"Really?"

"Yeah, but that's just a theory. No proof. We have to wait for the autopsy, forensics, and the detective's report."

"That should clear Shayla, though, right?"

"Yes, it should. We'll just have to wait to see what Detective Upton finds."

We sat in silence, listening to the splashing of water in the other room and I swear, I could hear Shayla crying. This wasn't going to be easy, but I was going to clear her of any wrongdoing, no matter what the police thought.

The water turned off, and a few minutes later, a clean Shayla came to join us.

"Feeling a little better?" I stood to greet her.

"Yeah, a little." She looked at Officer Perez. "I threw my old clothes out. I hope that's okay."

"Yeah, of course."

"I just wasn't sure if you would need them for evidence. They are in the trash back there." She gestured towards the shower area.

"Okay, I don't think we do, but I will let the detective know."

We walked back to the conference room to find Detective Upton standing against the far wall. Shayla made a sound and looked at me. I put my hand on her arm, trying to encourage her with a nod of my head.

"Detective," I greeted.

"Chef. Shayla." He flashed a flat smile. "Take a seat."

We followed his instructions. I took Shayla's hand as we waited to hear what he had to say.

"First of all, I am so very sorry for your loss."

Shayla mumbled something that sounded like thank you, but it was hard to hear.

"Then, I know you will want to know and to ease your mind, your sisters were picked up by their grandmother and she has taken them to her house," he said.

"Did you see them? Are they okay? Do they know what happened at home? Can I talk to them?"

"I'm not sure how they are. I didn't see them, but I believe she has told them or was going to tell them."

She bowed her head and made a choking sobbing sound. "They are going to be so sad. Ivy will start wetting the bed again and Dove will hide all the time. I need to talk to them."

"We can call after we leave," I assured her. She looked at me, nodding in acknowledgment.

"And how are you?" he asked.

"I'm okay. Numb mostly, but then I see her face ..." A lone tear slid down her face. "She tried to talk to me, to tell me who did it or what happened, but she couldn't."

"So, do you know what happened?" I asked Detective Upton.

"Well," he looked at me, then at Shayla. "You didn't see anyone?"

"No, nobody, but I heard the back door, or I think it was the back door, when I came in the front door. I didn't think anything of it at the time because there were always people coming and going. Then I found them, and I forgot all about it because I was focused on my mom and then the police arrived." Her voice cracked as she rushed to get all the words out. I squeezed her hand. She clenched it as if it was a lifeline, and perhaps it was.

"Why were you holding the gun?"

"I honestly don't know. I don't even remember picking it up until the officers yelled to drop it." She sobbed. "You don't think ... I just thought ... I didn't kill them."

"Okay. I am just trying to piece things together. Get a timeline." He looked at me. His stoic expression told me a different story than his words, but perhaps he was trying to be delicate with her.

"Yes, I had a problem with Mikey and my mom, but I didn't want them dead."

"Okay, okay. Not a problem. Do you know who might have?"

"I mean, it could be anyone. He wasn't a nice guy, and she wasn't exactly a joy either. Maybe one of their drugged-out friends or their dealer. Mikey owed him a lot of money."

"I have never heard of a drug dealer extending credit to people," Upton said, looking over at me. I shrugged.

"Yeah, weird, right? I don't know how it worked. I would just hear them arguing a lot about money."

"Do you have his name?"

"No, it was a nickname. Something like Boo or Bobo or Bob? I really don't know."

"Okay." He made a few notes in his little notebook. "I will track this. I think I know who you're talking about. Anything or anyone else you can think of?"

"No, nothing. I just want to talk to my sisters," she mumbled.

He nodded. "I'm so sorry, Shayla. I hope you will get to talk to them soon." He stood up, gesturing for us to follow him.

"Is that it? We are free to go?" I asked.

"Yes. I don't have any reason to detain you further." He paused, looking at me, then back to Shayla. "We have what we need. We'll be in touch."

We followed him out of the conference room. Officer Perez stood up from her desk. She handed Shayla her backpack and another bag, which might have been the things Shayla had gone to collect. Officer Perez then hugged her, whispering something in her ear. Shayla smiled flatly, nodding slowly as the hug ended.

With that, we continued out of the police station.

We didn't speak the entire drive home. She sat there quietly, sobbing as she stared out the window. I wanted ask how she was, but in that moment, she seemed like she needed to be quiet. I let her have that.

When we pulled in front of our townhouse, I saw that Vee and Sawyer were home. I hoped they had a plan for dinner, because I didn't. As we got out, the door opened, and Vee came through the door.

She hugged Shayla. No words, just a simple embrace. Sawyer came out, taking Shayla's bags. That was it. We all went inside and nothing else was said about today.

Chapter Three

The next morning, I stood in the kitchen sipping coffee, waiting for the griddle to heat and staring at Shayla's closed door. She was still sleeping. I wanted so badly to go wake her and see how she was doing.

Had she been able to sleep? The grief of losing her mother, the worry over her sisters, and with the police thinking she was a suspect had to be weighing heavily on her. Heck, maybe they still thought she was.

She wasn't going to school or work for a few days to allow her to grieve and process. Knowing that, it just seemed cruel to go wake her up. The rest would do her good.

So that she wouldn't be alone, I asked Parker to cover my shift for the next couple of days. I knew the worst thing would be if she got into her head about things. I would be here to distract her, listen, and just support her through this.

White and gray movement caught my eye on the stairs. It was Lulu. She pawed and meowed at the door. A few seconds later, the door opened a crack and Lulu went in.

Well, at least Shayla wouldn't be alone, I thought.

I turned to the griddle. It was ready for pancakes. I poured three blobs of batter and then watched as it started sizzling around the edge and bubbling in the middle. After a few moments, I flipped each of the beautiful round cakes.

"Perfect," I mumbled.

"Talking to yourself is a sign of insanity," Sawyer said, grabbing a coffee mug.

"Well, I have lived with you so long, it is a possibility."

"Ha, ha. I smelled something yummy." He came to watch me cook, setting his head on my shoulder.

"Pancakes and homemade sausage patties." I gestured to the plate with the perfectly cooked sausage waiting for us to bite into them. I liked mine dipped in sweet syrup.

I flipped the cooked pancakes onto a platter, then poured three more circles of batter.

"Any word from?" He thumbed towards Shayla's room.

"Not yet, but Lulu is in there with her," I said.

"That's good. Lulu is magical."

"She is. Helped me through a few things."

"Me too."

"Really?" I looked at him.

"Yeah, remember Stella?"

"Oh, yeah, I do." I flipped more pancakes to the platter. "She wasn't good enough for you." I added a wink.

"Yeah, well, at the time, it felt like I wasn't good enough for her." He grabbed a plate, piling it with the warm cakes. "Speaking of girlfriends, I have been talking with Riley about us possibly moving in together."

My heart stopped. I didn't want to live with Riley. I didn't hate her like I did in the beginning, but she still wasn't my favorite person. Home was the place I relaxed, but you just never knew what she was going to say.

"Oh?"

"Ha, yeah, I know, you aren't a fan, but don't worry, we've been talking about moving into her place. Plus, we have been dating for a while now and I never get to see her between my schedule and hers."

"That's nice." I didn't know what to say.

"Yeah, if we lived together, then we'd get to see each other more. Plus, I bought a ring."

"A ring?" I blurted.

"What ring? Who has a ring?" Vee's voice asked from the stairs.

"Jewelry." I laughed. "You hear talk about jewelry and nothing else?"

"I love jewelry, but seriously, what's this about a ring?"

"I got one for Riley. We're talking about moving in together and I think it is the right time for this."

"You want to break up our group?" Vee whined.

"I guess I am, but it isn't like we won't still be friends. Plus, it would give Shayla a place to live. She could take my room." He looked back and forth between us. "I am not going to do it if it leaves you both in a jam for my part of bills and rent, though."

There was a sudden smell of burning food.

"Oh, bleep!" I threw the burned pancakes out and started over.

"I can pay your part."

We all turned to see Shayla standing in the living room. Her red, puffy eyes told a story. She was holding a content Lulu. My cat, who hated to be held, looked happy as a clam in Shayla's arms. Maybe she just hated me holding her. Or, perhaps, she knew Shayla needed her.

Okay, that's the story I was going to tell myself, I thought. At least it didn't mean my cat hated me.

"We can't ask you to pay that much," Vee said.

"Why not? I graduate from high school in just a little over a month. I don't have a home any longer, so I will have to rent something." She took a seat at the kitchen island. "Why not somewhere that I already feel at home?"

Vee leaned over, wrapping her arms around her. That caused Lulu to jump down and run upstairs. We all laughed.

"I guess she only likes you." Vee giggled.

"Well, that doesn't make me feel loved." I laughed.

"She's a sweet cat." Shayla chuckled. "But seriously, I can pay my share of rent and bills. I have saved most of my money from the past months of working. I knew I couldn't stay at home much longer, anyway."

"Well, okay, if I decide to move out, you can have my room." Sawyer grinned. "Now, I need to decide if, or I guess when, this is really going to happen."

"What is holding you back?" I asked, as I flipped the last pancakes onto the platter.

"My own nerves. I never thought I would get this far with a girlfriend. I mean, it seems fast, but also it feels right. Ugh!" He groaned, then shoved a bite of pancake into his mouth.

"I didn't realize y'all were so serious, but I'm happy for you," I said.

"Thank you. You don't think I'm making a mistake?"

I had to think for a moment. Again, she wasn't my favorite person, but she seemed to make him happy. She seemed to get my friend. He was a special person, at least to me.

"Not at all! I think we all knew that we couldn't live together forever, right?" I said, looking at Vee for her confirmation.

"Yeah, absolutely!"

"Then that settles it." He chuckled. "I am going to ask her to marry me."

We all cheered and hugged him. Honestly, I was so happy for my friend, though selfishly, I would miss him being here with us. We wouldn't see him daily like we do now, but looking over at Shayla as she congratulated him, she needed us more. She needed a safe place, and this was perfect timing.

If I was honest with myself, I needed her, too. Something about her had brought out a different part of me. Something I hadn't even realized I had in me or knew I needed. It was that maternal instinct.

"We better get ready for work," Sawyer finally said.

"Oh, shoot, yes," Vee said, checking the time. She shoved the last bite of her breakfast in her mouth.

"I got your plate. Go!" I told her.

They ran upstairs. Shayla and I finished breakfast.

"I've got cleanup," she said.

"No, I can get it. Why don't you go call your sisters? I'm sure they would love to hear from you."

"Yeah, I need to." She started to head to her room. "Thanks, Jess. Your support in all this means so much."

"Of course. I've got your back."

She flashed a sad smile, then went into her room. I began cleaning the kitchen and trying to decide what we'd do all day to keep her mind and body busy. Maybe we could practice her éclairs for the 41st Annual Culinary Arts High School Competition.

This year's theme is Old Hollywood Glam. There were a lot of great ways to interpret that theme. For me, elegance, glamour, red carpet events, and award nights brought up the idea of having finger foods and small tasting bites. I'd probably do some bacon wrapped shrimp or maybe chicken meatballs.

I had no ideas for pastry. Thankfully, Shayla had a good mentor for that. She was working with my pastry chef, Natalie. They had been brainstorming. They had come up with a few ideas, but I don't know if they had it nailed down yet.

Shayla's raised voice coming from her room caused me to whip my head towards her door. Was she talking to her sisters like that? No, had to be the grandmother. I heard her voice change pitch, as if maybe she was crying.

Something in me snapped. I had to fight the urge to yell at whoever was on the other end of that call, even if it was the grandmother.

Instead, I finished wiping down the counters then got a fresh cup of coffee.

Vee and Sawyer came down. Vee came over to hug me.

"Who is she talking to?"

"I think her sister's grandmother."

"Not her grandmother too?"

"No, they have different fathers. This is their paternal grandmother."

I knew very little about Ivy and Dove's father, Ezra Lloyd, and even less about his mother, Lynn. What I did know about her, I didn't like.

"Was Mikey their father?" Vee asked.

"No, their father is Ezra Lloyd. Mikey was just their stepfather, like he was to Shayla, too."

She nodded in reply.

"You don't think that woman is taking out her anger on poor Shayla, do you?" Sawyer asked. His voice sounded like he was fighting the same battle I was.

It was crazy how we had all taken to her so quickly. She'd only been here about a month, but she was someone we were all ready to fight for.

"We need to get going but let us know if she needs anything," Vee said, hugging me again.

"I will."

They left for work.

I tried to busy myself, so it didn't seem like I was just hovering around, trying to listen in, even if I was. It was several minutes before her voice lowered and I could no longer hear her, but she didn't come out of her room.

I wasn't sure what else to do to keep busy, so I ran upstairs to grab my laundry. Then once that was going, I grabbed the broom to sweep our downstairs. When I finished and she still hadn't come out, I started mopping, then moved to reorganizing the kitchen.

It was more than an hour before she came out of her room. I was watching television and playing on my phone. Her eyes were red and puffy again, and my heart ached for what she was going through.

"Sorry, Jess." She plopped onto the couch next to me, laying her head in my lap. I started stroking her hair. It was something my Auntie Rita used to do to make me feel better.

Her hair was thick and soft. It wasn't when she first arrived. She shared with me that they didn't always have soap or water, so showers were rare. She'd sometimes visit a friend who was in the cosmetology program at the high school, and she would wash her hair for her. That made me both happy and sad for her.

"Are you okay?"

"No, but I will be." She smiled at me. "I know I already said it, but it can't be said enough, thank you for being so supportive."

"Of course. Want to talk about it?"

"Yeah, I guess." She made a strangled sound, tears in her eyes, but then sat up. "She wouldn't let me talk to them, even though I could clearly hear them in the background. She said I had done enough and didn't want to let me ruin the twins' lives any further. They have already been through so much. But I love them, too, and they are all I have left of family."

"What about your father?" I asked.

"He died years ago, when I was nine." She frowned. "I have my Aunt Harlow, though I haven't heard from her yet. I'm sure I will soon. She isn't exactly … um, available? I don't know if that's the right word, but just not there for me much. Though when she is, she is good to me."

"I get that." I had a few people that I might put in that category myself.

"Then there are random others, like cousins or other distant relatives, but nobody stepped up when I needed anywhere to go after Mikey hurt me. Nobody has come forward yet about my mom."

"I'm sorry." I tried to think of something to say. "You know I have a small family, too. My grandmother and aunt mostly. I have a mother, stepfather, and two half-brothers, but it's complicated. Most of my family are Vee and Sawyer, then everyone at The Crock Pot, which includes you. Found family is the best because they love you, not because they have to, but because they want to."

She smiled for the first time in nearly twenty-four hours.

"That … is awesome and so true." She laid in my lap again. "What happened to your family?"

"Oh, um," I hesitated slightly. I have told this story so many times. I was starting to feel somewhat disconnected from the actual events. It almost didn't feel real anymore, even though my father was in prison for it. "When I was five, my parents had people over for a party. One of the men touched me, in a not so appropriate way, and my father killed him. My mother then went into a deep depression, so I went to live with my grandmother and aunt."

"Oh, wow. I didn't know. So, what happened with your dad after that?"

"He's in prison for life. My parents got divorced before his trial and my mom remarried a year or so later. I now have two half-brothers who I hate."

"Oh, is he at Milton County?"

"Yes, he is."

"So is Ezra and I think I heard Mikey had been there, but honestly, I didn't pay much attention to him."

We sat quietly for a moment. I was thinking of how much of a coincidence it was that they were both where my dad is. I wonder if he knows them.

"I love my sisters, but they are little, so it's easy. How old are your brothers?"

"Chris is twenty and Bryan is eighteen."

"So, basically around my age."

"Yes, especially Bryan. He graduated high school this past June."

"Is he in college?"

"No, he works over at the hardware store. Only been a month or so now. Neither of them really worked before, so it's kind of a new thing."

"I wish Lynn would let me see my sisters. Ivy had just gotten over her bed wetting. Then Lynn isn't going to know how to find Dove when she hides. She does that when she gets upset, and she's really good at it. Sometimes I'm the only one who can find her and calm her down."

"It sounds like you have a good relationship with them."

"I think we do."

"What do you know about Ezra, their father?"

"Oh, there isn't much to say about him. Like I said, he's in prison. He went when the girls were just two years old, I think. Like Mikey, he had a hot temper, but it was mostly just yelling. He never hurt me or the girls. His mother, Lynn, was always around. Back then she treated me like one of her own grandchildren. It wasn't until he went to prison that she got hateful."

"I'm sorry."

Again, we sat there quietly, watching television, her head in my lap while I absently stroked her hair for nearly an hour without moving or talking. It was nice.

Her phone rang.

"Oh, well, look at that. My Aunt Harlow." She choked. "I better take this."

"Okay."

She answered it as she walked towards her room. I couldn't hear her this time. It must be a much calmer conversation. It broke my heart that she was struggling with all this and that she couldn't see her sisters. I would have to figure out a way to make that happen.

It was about ten minutes before she came back.

"She's planning my mom's funeral and wanted to tell me about it."

"Oh, when is it? Does she need you to do anything?"

"Next Thursday at ten a.m., and no."

"Okay, we will be there."

"Thanks, Jess. I really can't thank you and Vee and Sawyer for all the support." She wiped a tear. "I just want to know what happened. Do you think the detective has any more information?"

"Probably not. He would have called."

"Yeah." She hung her head for a moment, then looked at me. "Are we going to do the thing?"

She thumbed towards the office-slash-room she was staying in. Sawyer's dad had built us a large corkboard in there that we used as a murder board or clue board.

"Oh, um, I hadn't thought about it yet, but do you want to?"

"Very much so!" She darted into her room.

I chuckled and followed her. She was already writing on pieces of paper.

Victims: Mom. Mikey.
Suspects: Drug Dealers. Shayla.
Weapon: Gun

"Did you really put yourself down as a suspect?"

"Yeah, that's what the police think, so why not lean into it?"

"Because you didn't do it. Unless you are telling me you did?"

"No, of course not. I was at school then showed up a moment after it happened. My mom died in my arms." She frowned, but then pinned the victims note to the board. "I will never forget what her face looked like as she died."

She then pinned the next two papers, but she left her name off.

"Happy?" She grinned at me.

"Very."

"Do you think you became the Crime Fighting Chef because of what happened with your dad?"

I had never thought about that. Perhaps my pursuit of justice and finding the truth was because of watching my dad murder a man. Of course, it wasn't until thirty years later that I did solve my first murder mystery, but still, it could have formed some of my strong feelings about finding the killer.

"I never thought about it before, but maybe so."

We stood looking at the facts of the case. With no real clues yet, we couldn't do much.

"Well, it's a start," she said with a smile. "Maybe we should go to my house to look for clues."

"I don't think the police have cleared the scene yet, but maybe once they take down the crime tape."

"Okay. Sounds like a plan."

Chapter Four

The day had been fairly boring, which is just what Shayla had needed. In the evening, I received a text message from Officer Rafferty.

Why was he texting me? Did he have news on the killers?

R: **How's it going? How's Shayla?**

Me: **She's okay. We spent the day watching movies and trashy TV shows.**

R: **That sounds fun**

Me: **Any news on the killers?**

R: **Unfortunately, no.**

Me: **I guess it was just wishful thinking on my part that it would happen that quickly**

R: **I wish we would solve it fast. Shayla deserves that closure.**

Me: **Yes, she's the sweetest girl**

The three dots appeared showing he was typing, then they stopped. I guess he was done. Then they started again, and stopped, and then once more before I got his next message.

R: **So, the reason I'm texting, I wanted to see if you'd like to go to dinner with me.**

Me: **Like a date?**

R: **Yes**

I hesitated to reply. Was he serious? Wouldn't that be a conflict of interest of sorts? I was heavily invested in how this murder case turned out. It would be nice to be close to someone in the know. But did I want to go on a date with him?

It was dinner, not marriage, so a shared meal and some conversation with a longtime friend was a fun night. But I didn't have the best track record when it came to dating.

My phone rang. It was Raff. I guess I took too long to answer.

"Hello."

"Hey, did I scare you off? I'm sorry."

"No, no. Don't be sorry. I just … I have had bad luck with dating."

"I remember."

"That's not embarrassing to hear or anything." I laughed.

"Ha, sorry, I just meant I'd like to try."

"Do you think it would be a conflict of interest?" I asked.

"No, why? You're a chef and I'm a cop. Different jobs."

"Yeah, but what about the whole Crime Fighting Chef thing?"

"Well, hopefully that is over."

"Not until we find out who killed Shayla's mother and stepfather."

"Chief and Upton won't want to hear that." He laughed. I had always liked his laugh. It was deep and smooth.

"They probably won't, but if we go on a date or say we start dating or whatever, then what?"

"Then I think we'll both be happy and to hell with the other stuff," he said.

My mouth fell open. I'd only heard such cheesy things in movies, but it caused a flutter in my stomach.

"Um, yeah, when do you want to go?"

He chuckled. "What's your schedule like?"

I thought about Shayla. I wasn't ready to leave her for long. Vee would be here but was it the fair to leave her? I felt a lot of responsibility.

"Let me check and get back to you, okay?"

"Sounds good. We'll talk soon."

I fell back onto my bed with a sigh. It felt silly, but I had a date. Well, potential date. I giggled and rolled to my stomach.

"What's the giggling about?"

I jumped and rolled over.

"Oh, hey, Vee. Um, that's embarrassing. Where's the privacy?"

"If you wanted privacy, you should have shut your door."

"Good point." I sat up.

"Sooo, do tell. What was that about?"

"Um, it was nothing." I knew she wasn't going to buy it, and I could feel my face warming as she stared at me.

"Okay, if you want to lie to your very best friend, I will let you."

"Oh, the guilt trip. Fine. Sit, sit." I patted the bed. She giggled and leaped towards the bed, missing and falling to the floor.

We made eye contact and burst into laughter.

"You are the most graceful person." I reached down to pull her up, but we were laughing so hard we couldn't get her off the floor. In the chaos of my pulling, our laughing, and her falling back to the floor, somehow, I plopped to the floor as well.

We finally managed to right each other and get seated on the bed, but our laughter didn't stop.

Sawyer and Shayla came in.

"What's happening in here?" Sawyer asked.

"I heard a thump."

Vee and I burst into another round of laughter. I tried to calm down to tell them what had happened, but it didn't work.

Shayla's stoic face had us both sobering quickly.

"Sorry, she fell off the bed and when I tried to help her, I ended up on the floor," I said.

"It sounded like we missed a party." Sawyer chuckled. "But all good now?"

"Yeah, yes. We are fine." Vee sat on the bed. "She was going to give me some juicy gossip. I think you should both hear it, too."

"Wait? Good gossip?"

"Exciting." Shayla sat crossed legged on the floor.

"I was barely … I don't know."

"Oh, this must be about a guy. She has that look," Sawyer said to the other two.

"Yeah, she only looks like this when there is a guy," Vee giggled.

"A guy?" Shayla clapped her hands, then laid them in her lap.

"Fine. Okay. Fine. Raff asked me to dinner," I said in one hurried exhale.

"Ooohhhh!" they all said.

"He is cute."

"Too old for me, but I can see it."

"Not my type." Sawyer chuckled. "But he has asked me about you before."

"He asked about me?"

"Yeah, I'm glad he finally asked you out."

Shayla suddenly frowned. "Do you think, and I really hate to even think this, because it has been obvious for a while he likes you, but do you think the timing of now is because of … the murders?"

"What do you mean?" I had a feeling I knew exactly what she meant, but I hated to assume.

"Okay, but don't be mad. What if he just wants to do like that Todd guy did? Be close to you because of the investigation. You always seem to figure out who, either by drawing them out or putting the clues together. What if he is thinking now is a good time to get close to you so you can lead him to the killer?"

I felt like the wind was knocked out of me. I had thought about the conflict of interest where he knows information about cases and might slip telling me or having to keep those things from me. I hadn't thought of it going the other way.

"I hadn't thought of that."

"No, I'm sure he isn't doing that." Shayla smiled weakly.

"He has liked you for a while," Vee added.

"Yeah, he was asking about you before this, so I'm sure he isn't doing that," Sawyer said.

After what happened with Todd, it would be in the back of my mind with all future dates. Todd had only dated me to get close to my last investigation. It turned out to be one of his employees who was the killer.

Kyle Rafferty was at least someone I had known for a long time, since middle school, in fact. So, I felt I had a different level of trust with him. We had mutual friends, interests, and shared stories.

"Well, I agreed to go to dinner with him. We just have to figure out our schedules." I looked at Shayla. "I just don't want to leave you alone too much with everything."

"Don't worry about me. I have stuff to keep me busy," she said.

"And I'll be here with her." Vee smiled.

"Y'all sure?"

"Of course. Go. Any night."

"We are fine!"

"Plus, I will be here, except on Friday. Big night," Sawyer said.

"Wait? You set a date?"

"Friday?"

"Exciting!"

"Yeah, I decided to do this. I am going to ask Riley to marry me." He chuckled. "Wow."

"Congrats!"

"That's awesome."

"Yay! Happy for you."

"Now, back to you." He pointed. "When are you going on a date?"

I had actually hoped with Sawyer's news, they would forget about mine until I could think.

"Well, okay, I will talk to him again soon."

"How about … oh, I don't know … right now!" Vee laughed. The other two agreed.

They watched me as I sent him a text telling him any night this week worked. He replied asking about Wednesday night.

"Tomorrow? That's too soon, right?" I asked my audience.

"No, go!"

"You deserve this."

"That's perfect."

"Fine."

Me: **Tomorrow works**

R: **I'll pick you up at 6**

Me: **Sounds good**

"Okay, done. Date tomorrow at six." *Now what was I going to wear?*

With that settled, my friends said good night. I opened my eReader to my current book. After I'd read the same page five times, I went to my closet to pick out my outfit for tomorrow night. I flipped through my after work collection of outfits. It had grown slightly, as I wasn't working all the time.

I had gotten more of a work life balance the past month. I hoped it would continue. Maybe I could really return to the competition circuit, as I'd been thinking about lately. Though not to the extent I once was. Just a few each year.

I pulled out a black and silver cable-knit sweater, then pulled out a flowy boho skirt. This would go nicely with my chunky Mary Jane shoes and black tights. No, switch the skirt for skinny jeans.

Yep, that's the one.

"Okay, with that settled, maybe I can sleep now."

Chapter Five

The next day, after Sawyer and Vee went to work, Shayla started pulling out ingredients to work on her éclairs for the competition.

"Practice makes perfect is what Chef Nat has been telling me," Shayla said, as I sipped my coffee at the kitchen island.

"Mr. Jones used to say that, too."

"It's a good mantra." She smiled as she began measuring and adding the first components to the pot to boil.

"So, what's the plan here?"

"Well, after the pastry dough, the Choux, is in the oven baking, I'll make two fillings. One will be a chocolate cream and the other a coffee cream."

"That sounds good."

"Yeah, then I'll top the chocolate one with peanut butter ganache and the coffee one with a dark chocolate ganache."

"Those will be classy and glitzy enough to match the Hollywood Glam theme very well."

"I thought they might."

I watched her work. She was amazing to watch. It looked so easy, but I had never been good at baking. The Choux pastry wasn't even that difficult to make, but I always burned it up or under cooked it.

When she piped out the pastry, she was so even and smooth with her strokes.

"That's impressive," I commented. "You make it look so easy."

"It just takes patience and a steady hand."

"Not for me."

"You're one of the most patient people I know." She smiled at me. "I have heard such horror stories about working in the kitchen. Screaming, impatient, and fast-paced. Though your kitchen is fast, it isn't stressful, and the only yelling is just calling out orders or cheering for successful shifts."

"I have worked in a few kitchens that were nightmares. I wanted to create a different, more positive environment."

"I thought you only did competitions?"

"Not only. I had to get kitchen experience, too. I did about six to eight competitions a year, but the rest of the time, I worked in various kitchens. Since I didn't know what type of restaurant I wanted to open, I wanted to learn different cuisines and various styles."

"Smart."

"Yeah, it was great exposure to many things."

"Okay, these go into the oven for about twenty minutes."

She started mixing up the fillings and the ganache. At exactly twenty minutes, she pulled out the éclairs without even checking their doneness.

"Perfect," she mumbled as she began to transfer them to the cooling rack. Next, she filled and dipped them. "Ta-da!"

"They look gorgeous," I said, examining them. "So, are these the flavors you're going with for the competition?"

"I believe so." She handed me one of each flavor. "But what do you think?"

I took a bite out of the coffee cream and dark chocolate. It was rich and creamy. Then, I tried the peanut butter and chocolate one.

"Wow! I think they are awesome. Mr. Jones will love them."

"Oh, can we drop some off for him and Ms. Beverly?"

Beverly was his wife. She was a sweet lady and had always been involved with the school. Sometimes she even came in as a guest speaker.

"Yes, let's do it."

She clapped and got a container, filling it with two of each flavor. Then we both went to get dressed. I sent a message over to Mr. Jones, but I knew he was in class, so he likely wouldn't see it.

Once I was dressed, I headed downstairs. It sounded like Shayla was on the phone. I plopped down on the couch to wait. It was roughly fifteen or so minutes before Shayla emerged from her room. Her eyes were slightly red, but she didn't look like she was crying now.

"Sorry about that. My Aunt Harlow. The police have released the house, so she wants to get it cleaned out tomorrow."

"What's the rush?"

"Apparently, some development company wants that entire block."

It might be the same one my ex-boyfriend, if you could call him that, Todd, worked for.

I guess he had learned from his experiences with the Dashwood Beautification Organization that had tried killing him about a month ago. Actually, it wasn't the entire organization, just a few rogue members.

At the last city council meeting, I'd heard his company was buying up more abandoned and rundown areas to clean up. There were plans for affordable housing improvements, a park, and a community garden in that area.

The garden would be started by the company, all supplies provided and maintained by them. They would offer learning sessions on how to grow, keep, and harvest vegetables and fruits. It sounded like an excellent program. I really hope it took off.

"I've heard a little about their plans. It sounds like a good thing."

"I hope, but it will be kind of sad that my childhood home will be gone."

"What did you tell your aunt?"

"I told her I would meet her there and if you can't take me, I will order a rideshare."

"Of course, happy to drive you and can I help with cleanup?"

"Yes, I'd love it."

"Great. Ready to go?"

"Yes."

We loaded into my car and headed over to the school. As we drove, I tried to make small talk, but with each block, I could feel Shayla's energy changing. She simply sat, staring out the window.

Finally she turned to me, tears in her eyes.

"I'm not sure I can go into the school."

"Okay. Want to talk about it?"

"No," but she sighed. "It feels too normal. Everything just keeps moving around, but my life has fallen apart. Even the competition will go on and nobody will know my mother died."

"Oh, I'm so sorry. I was very young when my father was sent to prison, but I felt similar feelings. Life kept going, even though my home life had fallen apart. I had to keep going to school, church, and Girl Scouts."

"How did you get through it?"

"Honestly, I think my age had a lot to do with it. Plus, an amazing support system."

"You, Vee, and Sawyer have been wonderful through all this. Last month with Mikey, I thought that my life was over and then it wasn't. Now, I feel that kinda feeling again. Nothing will be normal, and my mother is gone. Even if she wasn't a great mother, she was my only one." She sniffled a bit, as tears slid down her face. "I know I already said that, but it's true. I'm an orphan at age seventeen."

That really hit me in the heart. It was awful to hear her say that. As much as my life had imploded years ago, I still had both of my parents. Though my mother was also not the best, she was the only mother I had.

Granny Ines and Auntie Rita were close to mothers, but they couldn't replace my mother. And as much as I wanted her to, Granny wouldn't live forever.

"Do you want me to keep driving to the school or do you want me to turn around?"

She let out a soft sob that sounded almost like a sigh.

"We can still drop them off, but could you go inside? I'll wait in the car."

"Of course. Whatever you need."

"Then can we go for a hike?"

"Absolutely."

Hours later, we were back home after dropping off the éclairs for Mr. Jones and then a two-mile hike. Even though we didn't talk much during the hike, when we got back to the car, Shayla had said it was just what she needed.

Now I was standing in my bathroom looking at my reflection.

Was I really going to dinner with Rafferty?

This seemed unreal. He was a longtime friend, and I hadn't thought of him as a potential date until Vee mentioned it a few weeks ago.

"Knock, knock," Vee said at my bedroom door. "You decent in here?"

"Yeah, in here," I said, still in the bathroom.

The door was partially shut, and she pushed it open fully.

"Well, don't you look nice."

"You think? I'm second guessing this outfit."

"No, that sweater with the skinny jeans looks great on you. Slimming."

I knew she was right about the slimming. This all black look did give the illusion of a smaller frame. I wasn't overweight exactly, just tall with a large build. My mother had always said that I was big boned.

There was a knock on my bedroom door.

"Hey, Jess, Officer Rafferty is here," Shayla said at the door.

"Oh, thanks." I looked over at Vee. "I'm nervous."

"You got this. You know him."

We headed downstairs. He was standing with Sawyer in the kitchen. They were leaning against the island. He looked nice in his casual clothing. It was just a simple button-down, long-sleeved shirt with dark blue jeans, but he looked nice.

I hadn't seen him in anything but his police uniform for years. We didn't exactly see each other socially.

He looked over and when he saw me, a wide smile spread across his face.

"Hey, Jess. Wow, you look ... amazing."

"Thanks. So do you."

"Ready to go?"

"Yes." I felt a flutter in my stomach.

"See ya, Sawyer." He nodded to Vee and Shayla as we walked out.

He opened the door to his truck for me, offering me his hand to help me in. I laughed a little mentally as I didn't really need the help, but it was nice.

"Thanks."

"Of course." He closed the door and ran around to the driver side. It gave me a few seconds to breathe and settle my nerves a bit. He smiled when he jumped in. "I have to admit, I'm a little nervous."

I laughed. "Me too. Silly, right? We've known each other forever."

"I know." He chuckled. He put the truck in gear, and we were off.

We made small talk as he drove us across town to Sushi 73. I wanted to ask questions about Mikey and Kenna's murder, but I knew I couldn't.

That was the conflict of interest I felt. Plus, it had only been a few days, they probably didn't have any new information.

"So, I know you probably want to know, but I don't have any new information about the case."

"Huh?" I wanted to ask if he could read minds, but I didn't.

"I just wanted to put it out there, in case you wanted to know. Nothing new yet, but I will say, we don't think Shayla killed them."

"Oh, well that's good."

"Sadly, she is still on the suspect list, but we all don't believe it was her."

"I don't understand how that works. Either she is or isn't a suspect."

"True." He looked quickly at me as he pulled into the lot. "I just mean none of us believe she was the one, so we aren't actively looking at her as the suspect and are looking for the real person."

That made almost no sense, but I overlooked it for now.

"Any news on the drug dealer? Did y'all figure out his name?"

"Not yet. We have a few. It could have also been one out of Pinehurst. It happens."

I nodded. There was often crime that seeped over here from Pinehurst.

He parked and we headed inside. I rarely ate in the restaurant at Sushi 73, even though it was one of my favorites. I preferred it as take out.

Chef Kano was a friend. We had gone head to head in a competition once years ago. It was a hometown theme. He won that round and never let me forget it.

It was a friendly rivalry.

Stepping into the modern restaurant with glass and neon everywhere was a stark contrast to my own homestyle restaurant with all the local artwork on the walls. This was definitely Kano's style.

"Jess!" He yelled from behind the all-glass counter. He was slicing a roll into neat, even pieces. "Welcome! And Officer Rafferty? Well, well, is this a date?"

I was thankful for all the bright colored neon masking the blush on my face when Kano asked us that. This is how rumors got started. I mean, it was true, but still, I didn't want people talking about my love life. My restaurant yes, dating life no.

"Yes, it is," Kyle said in his booming voice. "Finally, I got the nerve to ask."

"Well, that's awesome. Have a seat anywhere you like. Suzy will be right with you." Suzy was his wife, as well as the server and cashier.

We took a seat against the front window. It gave us a good view of the street. Suzy came to take our order. She smiled and gave me a little wink as she walked away.

Making small talk was easy enough, we knew all the same people, had many of the same experiences, and a lot in common. Unlike other dates, there were no awkward pauses or breaks. It was just two people who already knew each other well, enjoying conversation and good food.

There was no more talk about the case, and honestly, I didn't even think about it again. I knew he wouldn't have much to give, even if he could.

Later, on the front steps of my townhouse, we said good night.

"I'd like to do it again sometime, if you'd like that," He said.

"I'd love to."

"Great. I'll text you soon." He leaned forward, giving me a quick kiss and a hug. "Good night, Jess."

"Night, Kyle."

Chapter Six

I woke with a smile and a good morning text from Kyle. I replied then laid there grinning. It was a good date. Maybe my bad luck with dating was finally behind me.

Pushing myself up, I needed to get moving. We would be heading over to Shayla's old house. It was clean up and clean out day with her Aunt Harlow. I knew Shayla was not looking forward to this.

Vee had taken the day off to help us, too. Sawyer was saving his days off for his upcoming move to Riley's place, though he wasn't sure when that would be yet. He just kept saying soon, but he was still planning on his special dinner tomorrow night.

Once we were all ready, we gathered boxes, tape, scissors, and trash bags, loading those into my car. It would make the process easier. Though I remember there wasn't much in the house other than garbage, so we would probably end up using mostly trash bags.

When we arrived, Harlow wasn't here yet, so Shayla unlocked the door. We walked into eerie silence, dank air, and an acrid moldy smell. It was not going to be pleasant.

We stood there a moment, waiting for Shayla to give us a direction or make a move.

"It's so quiet without the television, Mikey's yelling, or my sisters giggling in their room," Shayla finally said.

She walked tentatively into the living room, turning on the lights and switching on the ceiling fan. It helped with the air and the smell, but only to a point.

"Where should we start?" I asked.

"Clues would probably be in their room. I really wasn't allowed in there, so likely that's where things would be."

"Okay."

She took the lead down the hallway to the last door on the left. There was a large, lumpy mattress on the floor. No box spring or support of any kind. The sheets had either been removed or perhaps they didn't have any. There was a blanket thrown to one side.

It was easy to tell that Gail and the rest of the police department's cleaning crew had been here, though they had only cleaned up where there had been blood, as there were strange clean spots mixed into the dingy areas of the carpet, walls, and the mattress.

And if you happened to not notice the weird clean spots mixed among the filth, there was the strong bleached-chemical smell that burned the nose and throat. It was a telltale sign that the professional cleaners had been here, but only for a specific job. Nothing more.

Shayla didn't move, just looked around from the doorway.

"I can do this," Shayla mumbled, barely audible.

I knew this was going to be hard for her to relive and stand in the place where she watched her mother die in her arms. I touched her arm gently, giving it a light squeeze of encouragement. She gave a half-smile in reply.

We began looking around in drawers and in the closet, but there wasn't a lot. Clothes in the closet were mostly t-shirts. Yoga pants and cargo shorts in the drawers. We checked pockets.

"Gum wrapper, a gas station receipt, and a lighter is all I found in here," Vee said, holding the items.

"Nothing in the closet. No pockets." I shrugged, turning.

"A pack of cigarettes, more lighters, and a vape pen in this night stand, but nothing else. I guess the police took any drugs that might have been here. Maybe their cell phones too."

"Okay, so no clues here," I said.

That's when I noticed something sticking out from under the mattress. I almost missed it. As I pulled it out, they turned to watch me. My eyes widened as I read the three words.

"I warned you," I read it out loud.

Shayla made a strangled sound as her face paled.

"Whoa," Vee said.

"Well, that's a clue, but I have no idea who or what or why."

"Yeah. Probably sent by who killed them, but it doesn't give us a name," Vee said.

Shayla stared straight ahead, then walked into the hallway.

"Should we look under the mattress to see if there is anything else?" Vee asked me.

"I'll lift, you look?"

She nodded. I pulled the mattress up, and a roach ran out. Vee jumped back with a slight squeal. Unfortunately, there was nothing else under it. I let it drop back down, then we joined Shayla in the hallway.

She was staring at a room across the hall, almost frozen in place. I couldn't see into it from where I stood, but I assumed it was her sisters' room. She finally walked in, looked around, then walked out.

That's when we heard a car door outside, so we quickly made our way back to the living room. I shoved the paper deep into my pocket just as a bubbly, loud woman stepped in.

"Hello?" she said, looking around. Her eyes locked on Shayla. "Oh, Shayla, dear." She rushed to her, wrapping her in her arms. "I'm so very sorry. You, Ivy, and Dove did not deserve this."

"I'm sorry, too. You lost your sister."

"Bah, she was not much of a sister to me. Not for years. I already mourned that loss."

Vee and I exchanged a look. I didn't want to seem judgy, so I kept my mouth shut.

I didn't have a sister or even a sibling close to me. I think I sometimes romanticized that relationship. When I saw people who had a sister or sibling relationship that they took for granted, it always brought up my feelings of longing for what I feel I missed out on.

My half-brothers, Bryan and Christopher hated me, and they had each other, so what did they need me for?

I studied Harlow. Shayla had told me she was only a few years older than me, but she looked much older. Unless I actually looked this old, too. I fought the urge to touch my own face.

Hers was creased with fine lines and had a weathered look to it, like she had spent too much time in the sun. Her amber-brown hair was pulled into a high ponytail. She wore a small crop top, yoga pants, and expensive sneakers. It was like she was trying to hold on to her youth, but her skin gave it away.

She also didn't look much like her sister, though I'd only met Kenna a few times. Perhaps I was remembering her wrong.

From my brief meeting with her, Kenna had looked frumpy and rundown all over, not just in her aging face. From her dishwater-colored hair to her dull blue eyes down to her cheap flip-flops she always seemed to have on.

"Oh, I'm so sorry." Harlow turned towards us. "I'm Harlow. Kenna's sister and Shayla's aunt. You must be Jess and Vee."

"Yes, I'm Jess."

"Thank you for taking our Shayla in like this. I would take her myself, of course, but you know how these things are. I have my four kids and a husband. Plus, a full-time job. The kids keep me running from dawn to dusk and beyond."

"Ah, yeah." Though I didn't understand. I might not have children or a husband, but I was running my own business. Plus, Shayla was her flesh and blood, why not help her out?

I loved having Shayla, though, so I wouldn't complain.

"Where should we start?" Harlow asked.

We looked at each other as if we hadn't already been snooping around.

"Is Grandma Lynn going to pick up the girls' things?" Shayla asked.

"I didn't call her."

"Why not? She should know so they can get Ivy and Dove's things. They will want them."

"You can call her. I will start with Kenna's clothes." She pulled out a roll of garbage bags and snapped one open. "I doubt anyone will want this stuff."

Shayla looked at me, her mouth wide open. Not sure what she liked about her aunt. She was a bit rude.

"Okay, I'll call her, but worst case, I will take their stuff with me." She pulled out her phone. "Um, maybe y'all can start in the kitchen? Pack anything usable. Toss anything that's food or trash. Though I expect you'll find more trash than food. I'll be in there once I'm done with Grandma Lynn."

Vee and I headed into the kitchen. It was how I expected, full of trash. Bugs scurried away as we flipped on the light.

"Blah. I can't believe they were living in this," Vee whispered.

"I know. It makes me sad, but also happy that we're able to take her in."

We each slipped on gloves, then snapped a trash bag open and got to work. I am so glad I thought to bring gloves. Vee started in the cabinets, and I started in the fridge.

It was a few minutes before Shayla came in. By the look of her eyes, she had been crying again.

"She doesn't want to have their stuff. Says they need to forget this life and move on."

"I'm sorry."

"That's crazy," Vee said with a sympathetic smile. "Do you want to forget this life?"

"No. It wasn't the best, but it has made me who I am. I'm strong. I'm capable. Why? Because I wanted better than this. Plus, I love my sisters. They were my favorite part of this chapter of my life and now she won't let me see them or even give them their things."

"What do you want us to do for you?"

She looked around. "Let's just get this place cleaned up. I will take their things with me. It isn't a lot, but it should be saved for them."

"Well, alright."

We got back to work. Shayla went to clean her sisters' room and help Harlow while Vee and I continued in the kitchen. It was mostly junk, and after an hour, we had filled five trash bags and two boxes with dishes. The latter would be donated.

"I got the master bedroom cleaned up. Eight bags of trash. Not saving anything from there," Harlow said.

"Except for the couple of shirts I grabbed," Shayla added. "The only things I want to save of my mom's."

"What about your room?" I asked her.

"I took everything to your place already, except this one box." She held the one in her arms higher. "I'm finished in the girls' room but just need to take their things to the car."

"That just leaves the bathroom," Vee said.

"Yes, and I have a junk removal company coming for everything tomorrow. If we just pile up the trash in here, they will get it all."

"Great. We will get this wrapped up," Vee said.

"Wait? What about their car?" Shayla asked. "Can I have it?"

I saw it in the driveway. It was a maroon Chevy Malibu. I didn't know much about cars, but it looked like an older year,though still in decent condition.

Harlow looked at her, studying her for a moment before answering. "Yeah, I don't see why not. I will work with the lawyer to get the title transferred to you once I get the death certificates. The sale of the house will be split between you and your sisters."

Shayla's mouth fell open. "Really? I thought you ... I didn't know how that worked."

"Yeah, I told the lawyer that was the right thing, but I can't imagine it will be much. Still, it will be something for you to live on and Lynn will likely put it for college or whatever for Ivy and Dove."

"Thank you."

With that, we all got back to work. There wasn't much to save in the bathroom, not that there was much in there. Half a dozen shampoo and conditioner bottles in various states of emptiness went straight into the trash. Threadbare towels, a bleach-stained bath mat, and a bunch of random makeup followed it. Four trash bags later, we were done.

We dragged all the trash bags into the living room, stacking them with the others. We helped get the things Shayla wanted to keep loaded into my car.

"Alrighty, I think that's pretty much everything. It didn't take as long as I thought it would." Harlow checked her watch. "I should have time to grab a Chai tea before picking up my kids from school. The girls have dance, and Henry has basketball practice, so I will be on the go, go, go. I'll need that tea." She stretched her arms out, gathering Shayla in them. "Thank you so much for helping. Keep in touch and I will see you next Thursday at the service, yes?"

"Of course. Oh, did you ask Grandma Lynn?"

"Yes, that I did tell her about. She says they will be there."

"Okay."

"And, I'll let you know once I get the car moved into your name. Until then, take it with you." She pulled the keys out of her purse, tossing them to Shayla.

"Oh, wow, thanks. This is going to help me so much." She turned to me grinning. "No more begging for rides."

"Yay!"

"Well, I'm out," Harlow said. "Nice to meet you both. Thank you."

She waved as she jogged down the walkway to her giant SUV at the curb. It made sense since having four kids that she needed all the space.

"Race you home!" Shayla giggled as she ran to her car.

Chapter Seven

Friday meant both Shayla and I were getting back to our normal life. She would be going back to school then work after, and I would work the day shift.

She bounced out of her room, jingling the keys to her new-used car.

"I'm so excited to drive myself to school today!" She laughed. "I mean, it doesn't exactly lessen the grief, but it helps a little bit."

"I get it. You deserve it."

She frowned. "I really do hate that they were killed, especially my mom. I just don't want to seem selfish or bratty for being happy about the car."

"I get it. I'm definitely not judging you."

"Do you think people at school will? At work?"

I realized what she was saying. I came around the kitchen island, setting my coffee down as I did. When I reached her, I wrapped her into my arms.

"No, nobody will think that. Anyone who knows you knows that you are a wonderful person. Caring, generous, and loving. You really do deserve to have good things in your life. Sometimes bad stuff has to happen first." I kissed the top of her head. "You are going to do great things."

She grinned up at me. The kiss might have been over the top with just any employee, but she had become like a little sister or almost a daughter. It felt right and she seemed to appreciate it.

"Okay. I just feel a little guilty that I'm kind of happy. I just feel safer now." Her voice came out weakly.

"You are safe, and you can feel however you want."

"Thank you. I needed to hear that."

"That's what I'm here for." I gave her a light squeeze before letting her go. "Alright, ready for some breakfast? I made omelets."

"Sausage and peppers?"

"Of course."

"Yum. Thanks."

Vee and Sawyer joined us minutes later, then one by one, we all headed out for our day. I was the last to leave. It gave me time to go into Shayla's room to look at the murder board. It felt a little weird going in there without her home, but she had told me it was okay many times.

We hadn't added much to the board, which I hated, but it had only been a few days since their murder. When we got home yesterday, I tacked the warning note to the board, adding a post-it note with a huge question mark on it.

I also hadn't heard anything from the police.

Would they tell me anything?

Probably not, and I wasn't going to pester Raff with a bunch of questions. It wasn't right and I didn't want to put him in the middle.

Detective Upton hated when I nosed around in police business, but they were slow to find the killer. I hated to wait, and the past cases were personal to me. This one was equally as important. She had no one and nobody to hold her up.

I took one more look at the board, but with nothing much on it, there wasn't much I could do. I headed upstairs to get ready for work.

It felt good to be back in the kitchen. Almost like when you finally reach that itch you haven't been able to scratch.

"We sure missed you around her, Chef," Hannah said, after our lunch rush was down to a near stop.

"I missed it too. Thanks for helping out."

"Of course."

"Which leads me to my next question, or really a statement, I guess." I looked over as Noah walked up. He knew what I was going to ask and already had the paperwork worked up. I took the paper from him, handing it to Hannah. "We'd like to offer you a promotion to sous chef, which means you and I would be switching days off and on. Eli will be taking your place as the line cook for day shift."

"Oh, my gosh! Oh, Chef! Are you sure? You think I'm ready?"

"I do. You have been kicking butt around here."

"What will you do?"

"What I probably should be doing, taking more of a manager role, by developing employees and developing new menu items. Things like that."

"And days off," Noah added. "For you and me."

"Yes, days off, too."

Hannah was reading the letter, then looked up. "Do I sign this or just, what do I do?"

"Yeah, let's go in the office. I'll get you a copy once it's signed." Noah said, thumbing towards the office.

I smiled as I watched them walk away. We got a new order, so I started working on it. It was shrimp and grits, a cheeseburger with fries, and the soup of the day, which was potato leek.

"Need an order of fries," I yelled.

"Got it, Chef," Eli replied.

Minutes later, I slid the plates into the pickup window.

"Runner!"

Marco came up, grabbing them with a huge grin. "Got it, Chef."

"Thanks, Marco," I smiled.

I was so glad to have him back to his happy self. A little more than a month ago, he had lost a friend and fellow veteran in an awful murder. If that wasn't bad enough, he was the prime suspect. Luckily, I was able to find the real killer and clear his name.

I watched as he took the plates of food into the dining room with a little bounce in his step. It made me smile even brighter. It was a good feeling to give him his life back. Of course, he was still doing therapy through Veteran's Affairs.

"I'm having the best day," I whispered to myself.

"What's that, Chef?" Eli asked.

"Just having a good day. How about you?"

"Definitely a good one. Thanks for asking." He smiled, then turned to wipe down his station and get it ready for the next orders.

We had to hire more staff due to an increase in business, and Eli was part of that hiring spree. He'd only worked here a few weeks. We also had a few new servers and bussers as well.

Hannah came back with a huge smile on her face, going to her station. A new order came back, but then my phone rang. It was Shayla. My stomach churned. She was a texter unless something was wrong.

"I got ya, Chef," Hannah said, taking the order.

I stepped away as I answered it.

"Shayla, what's wrong?" The mama bear side of me I didn't even know I had was engaged.

"I keep getting weird text messages today and I think someone is following me." Her voice was almost shrill.

"Where are you?"

"Two blocks from home."

"Turn and go to the police station. I'll call Raff to see where he is, and I will meet you there."

"Okay."

"Do you want me to stay on the phone with you?"

"Yes, but then how are you going to call Raff?"

"Oh, right? Let me see if Noah is busy, but I'll stay on the phone."

I walked towards the office. No Noah.

"He isn't in here. I'm walking to the dining room. Is the car still following you?"

"Um, yes. Yes, it is. There's a car between us, but it's still there."

"Then how do you know it's following you?"

"Because I turned randomly, and it has stayed right with me. I even backtracked a bit. Then I did a U-turn and so did that car. I don't know if they know I know, but it's scary."

"Okay. Okay." *Yes, that didn't sound right.* "I found Noah. One sec." I filled him in.

"Crap, yeah, let me call. Hold on."

He pulled out his phone from his pocket to dial, as we walked to the office. I heard him talking to Rafferty, nodding to me as he spoke.

"Okay, so you'll meet her in the parking lot? Okay. I'll tell Jess."

My stomach fluttered at the thought of seeing him, then it churned a bit as I thought of Shayla in trouble. What a mix of emotions!

"Tell him I'm on my way, too," I mouthed.

"Jess says she's on her way." He waved to me. I grabbed my purse and sprinted out.

I talked to Shayla for only another minute or so, until she arrived at the police station. Thankfully, the restaurant was only a few blocks away from there.

When I got to the station, I saw her car parked in the visitor lot, but no sign of her or Rafferty. I parked next to her and jogged inside.

"Jessica, right?" the officer at the desk asked.

"Yes."

"I'll buzz Raff. Have a seat."

A minute later, the door opened, and Officer Roberts called me back.

"Where is Raff?" I asked.

"He's interviewing Shayla."

"Interviewing? Why? What happened?" I knew she'd been followed, that's why I told her to come here, but interviewing sounded much more serious. I hope she wasn't hurt.

"Just getting the texts and a description of the car."

"Okay, that makes sense." Me panic for no reason? Never.

We walked through the bullpen and to the same conference room that we were in days ago. Several officers watched as we passed. Officer Perez flashed me a smile.

Roberts knocked on the door, pushing it open.

"Jess is here."

"Come in, Jess," Rafferty said. He was frowning until we locked eyes, then his beautiful smile spread across his face. "Hi," he said softly.

"Hi." I then looked at Shayla. Her eyes were red, but she was in one piece. "You okay?"

"Yeah, and at least I know what to do if it happens again." She looked up at Rafferty.

"Good. So, what do we know? Were you able to catch them on CCTV?" I asked Raff.

"Yes, but no plate. They had a paper one. We have Officer Wright doing a search then Roberts and I will be going to drive around as soon as I'm done here."

"Oh, great, so by then they will have time to put a plate on their car, if they have one. Or perhaps they will have it parked in a garage." I had seen enough true crime to know that both were possible.

"I guess, but we have to try and if we find a car that even matched the one following her, we will have a good look at them."

"Okay, what do we need to do?"

"Nothing, just stay alert, like she was, and stay safe, please." He stood up. "I think I have everything I need from your phone and I have your statement, so you are good to go."

"Thank you," she mumbled.

"Thanks, Raff. Please let us know when you find something," I said.

"I will." He smiled. "I'll walk y'all out."

We walked back out to the parking lot.

"I'll call you later," he whispered to me.

"Okay." I smiled at him.

He stood at the doorway watching us get in our cars, then waved as we drove away. I pulled out behind Shayla so I could keep an eye on her.

She would go home to change before heading to work. But to make sure she was safe, I would call Cullen to make sure that she didn't leave alone tonight.

"I'm going to write weird text messages and stalker, then put that on the board," she said, once we were in the house.

"Good idea. But really, you're okay?"

"Yes, I'm okay. They didn't really do anything. Oh, but I didn't show you the texts."

She tapped on her phone and then handed it to me.

They were from a blocked number.

1st one: **U got lucky**

2nd one: **U R taking the fall**

3rd one: **Watch UR back**

4th one: **Ha, JK**

"Wait does this JK mean, just kidding?"

"Yeah, I guess so. That's all I can come up with and Officer Rafferty, Roberts, and Perez thought the same."

"Was this person just harassing you? Trying to scare you?"

She shrugged. "Who knows?"

I looked at them once more before handing her the phone. She took it then went to get dressed. I took this time to call over to the restaurant.

"Hello, The Crock Pot restaurant." Noah's voice came through the line.

"Noah? I didn't think you'd still be there."

"Oh, yeah, Cullen just got here, and we were starting to do turnover."

"Ah, okay. I wanted to talk to him."

"Okay, but hey, how is Shayla?"

"She's fine but I wanted Cullen to watch out for her tonight."

"Of course, that makes sense. Here."

"Hey, Chef, what's up?" Cullen asked.

When I heard his voice, I had an idea pop into my head.

"Okay, so two things. One, please watch Shayla. Don't let her go out alone and when it is time to leave, have someone escort her."

"Of course, we all leave together. No one leaves alone but I will be extra careful with watching her."

"Thank you. Okay, the other thing, do you think you can hack into the city security cameras?"

"Of course I can. You know I do more than spreadsheets."

"Ha, yeah, I know that now. You were a lifesaver with Marco's case."

"It was my pleasure to help him out. What am I looking for?" Cullen asked.

"Footage of the car that was following Shayla. I want to know if you can trace where it went and see if you can figure out who the driver was. All of it."

"Can do. It might take a day or two, but I will get that for you."

"Thanks so much. Have a good evening."

"Later."

I stared at the phone for a moment, then I laughed at myself. In movies or television shows, you always see people do that and it seemed so silly, but here I was staring at my phone.

Setting it on the counter, I went into the kitchen to start prepping dinner.

Tonight, it would just be Vee and I as Shayla would be at work and tonight was Sawyer's big date with Riley. The one where we lose our best friend and roommate to his girlfriend.

It was bittersweet but overall, I was glad my friend found his person. If only I could find mine.

You might have already met him, I thought. *Ha, maybe I had.*

As I was chopping veggies and lettuce for our big salads, what I had planned for Vee and me, Shayla came out of her room.

"Okay, I'm out."

"I'll walk you to your car."

"Really? Are you going to be all paranoid on me?"

I stared at her for a split second. Did she not understand what just happened? After I did a quick count to ten, as I gathered my thoughts, I reminded myself she was still a kid. Even if at times she seemed more mature than her age. She was, at the end of the day, a kid.

"Yes, I will be paranoid on you. You received harassing texts. You were followed, and you found your mother and stepfather executed just days ago." I paused to think of what else to say. "I also called Cullen, and he will be watching you carefully too. We all want you safe."

"Fine." She sighed as she stomped towards the door.

I followed and watched as she climbed in. She hooked up her phone to the Bluetooth, adjusted things, turned on the music, then finally, finally pulled from the curb.

During her whole routine, I kept my head on a swivel taking in any movement, even the stray cat as it crept through the bushes across the street. He stared at me, then went back to cleaning himself.

I stood there until she turned the corner and disappeared from sight. I had to trust she was safe and would pay attention to her surroundings, just as she had after school.

A car came from the opposite street and pulled to a stop in front of our house. It was Vee and Sawyer.

"Hey, what are you doing out here?" Vee giggled as she got out of the car. "Miss us that much?"

"Yes, ha, but that's not why I'm out here." I looked up the street. "Shayla just left for work."

"Oh, nice. How was her first day back at school?" Vee came over, hugging me.

"It sounded good until it wasn't."

"What do you mean?" Sawyer asked.

I looked around. The stray cat was the only other living thing on the street. He had given up cleaning himself and was now hunting something. But to avoid being heard, I thought we should go inside.

"Let's go in to talk about it."

They nodded and we all headed in. I let out a sigh.

"Someone sent her a bunch of harassing texts about her mom's death and then she had a car following her after school."

"What?"

"Are you serious?"

Vee gasped as I told them about everything from the moment Shayla called me until the conference room with Rafferty. Repeating it made me want to chase after her and keep her by my side.

"Is this what motherhood is?" I mumbled absently.

"I think so, and I am feeling very big brotherly or fatherly. I want to beat someone," Sawyer growled. "Don't mess with our girl."

"Me too," Vee said.

"I did ask Cullen to keep an eye on her."

"Who else works nights that can protect her?"

"Maybe Crosby? He isn't as large as Marco, but he is strong."

Crosby was one of my evening servers. He was a charming guy who was really good with the customers. Though he had a shady past, I had always believed in second chances, and he had done his time.

"Crosby, right? I would trust him to protect me" Vee said with a giggle. I looked at her as she touched her quickly reddening checks.

"Oh my gosh, are you serious? Crosby?"

"What? He is *cute.*"

"Well, I better go get ready for my date," Sawyer said.

"Good luck!"

"We love you."

He ran up the stairs leaving Vee and I sitting at the kitchen island.

"I was thinking big salads for dinner."

"Awesome. I'll go change then I can help with whatever you need," Vee said.

Hours later, I was in bed wide awake. I wasn't going to be able to sleep until I knew Shayla was safe in the house. My phone chimed.

S: **On my way. Cullen is following me home**

Me: **Great!**

Thankfully, she got home uneventfully and went to bed almost immediately. I laid in my bed being oh so thankful.

Chapter Eight

"Hurry up, y'all! Ms. Ines promised her albondigas soup and tamales for me!" Sawyer yelled.

"What is albon-digas?" Riley asked.

"Meatballs," I said.

"Oh, I love meatballs." Riley giggled. She held her left hand out, looking at the new ring on it.

My friend had really good taste. It wasn't a traditional diamond engagement ring. Instead, it was their birthstones set on either side of a diamond. It was so romantic and thoughtful. Who knew?

"Vee! Come on!" Sawyer said, tapping his foot. Shayla giggled at my side. He looked over at her.

"What?" she asked with an innocent shrug.

"I take Ms. Ines's food very seriously."

"Obvs!" She laughed.

Vee finally came down. "I'm sorry. My hair, again."

"It looks great," Shayla said.

"Thanks, but it took a lot of time to get it like this."

"Alright, are we ready?"

But before we could leave there was a knock at the door. We all looked around. I counted each of us. There wasn't anyone else we were expecting.

"Who could that be?" Sawyer asked. He was closest to the door, so he answered.

"Is Shayla here?" the man at the door asked.

"Uncle Jay? What are you doing here?" She walked towards the door, crossing her arms hard over her chest. The protective side of me snapped to attention.

I remember Shayla mentioning him. Jay was her stepfather's brother. She'd mentioned he was as mean as Mikey and had recently gotten out of prison.

"I've come to check on you." He stepped forward, but Sawyer stood a little straighter causing Jay to take a step back. I guess he could hear the defensiveness in Shayla, too.

"I'm *fine.*"

"Good, good." He looked at us. "Is there somewhere we could talk in private?"

"No, here is fine."

He nodded. "So, um, did the police give you any idea of what happened?"

"No, not really."

"No ideas who murdered my brother?" He snapped a little, causing her to take a small step back. The rest of us stood solid beside her.

"None yet." Her voice wobbled a bit. "They are working on it. I tried to think of anyone who would want to hurt them, but I couldn't come up with anyone."

"You told them about Bobo, right? Ole Mikey owed him like thousands. I'm sure Bobo came a knockin' for that dough."

"Bobo! That's his name. I couldn't come up with his name."

"So, you did tell them that name?" Jay asked, stepping forward again. Sawyer puffed up a bit, ready for whatever was happening. "Calm down, cowboy. I am just talkin' to her."

"I'm calm. You stay calm," Sawyer said.

"I'm calm, man. Calm as a cucumber."

"I think it's cool as a cucumber," Riley said.

"And who are you?"

"His girlfriend ... err, no fiancée."

"Yeah? Well, I'm *her* uncle."

"Step-uncle," Shayla corrected. His head snapped to stare at her.

"Really, Shay, after all I've done for you?"

"What have you done for me? Helped Mikey beat me? Torture me?"

"I never ... I mean ... I—"

"We need to go, Uncle Jay but thank you for stopping by." She said it with such confidence and force that we all looked at her to make sure it was still Shayla. Her arms were still crossed, and her lips pressed tight.

"Okay, but one more question."

"Okay, fine."

"Do you think it could have been Ivy and Dove's father?"

"Ezra?"

"Yeah, Ezra. He hated Mikey being around his girls. They got in a huge fight a month or so ago. It was bad."

"How did they fight? Ezra is in prison," I said.

"It was over the phone. Then Trina came to get the girls for a visit with Lynn. Kenna and Trina got into it right there in the yard."

The blank looks on our faces must have triggered Shayla to explain.

"Trina is Ezra's girlfriend. She lives with Grandma Lynn."

"Ah. Okay," we all said in near unison.

"Yeah, Trina is a whore and hated Kenna. I think she feeds lies to Ezra to fan the flames of the feud," Jay said, taking a step down the steps. "But alrighty, y'all. I will head out because Shay said I needed to."

"Bye," Shayla said, flatly.

We stood there watching him walk down the block. He didn't get into a car but turned at the end of the block.

"You okay?"

"Yeah, yeah. I'm … I'm fine."

Vee touched her arm. "You sure?"

"I'm not at the moment, but I will be. He creeps me out."

"Did he really take part in abusing you?" I asked her.

"Yeah, but mostly just laughing and would sometimes kick or swat at me as Mikey did the rest."

"I'm sorry," Vee and I said together.

"Well, let's get going." She wiped her eyes. "Ms. Ines will have our hides if we are late."

We laughed then piled into Shayla's car. It was a bit of a squeeze for us in the backseat, but Riley didn't seem to mind snuggling against Sawyer. I felt like a third wheel sitting back there with them. Vee got to sit in the front.

I had never been in the car with a teen driver, at least not since I was one, but Shayla did great. I felt completely safe.

We pulled up at Granny's house one minute late. Granny was standing in the doorway tapping her foot, arms crossed. I had seen that stern look on her face many times over the years.

"She's not happy," Sawyer mumbled with a laugh as we all climbed out.

"Sorry, Granny. We had an unexpected visitor," I said when we got to the door.

"Hmph, you could have called." She pushed the screen door open for us.

"We should have. I'm sorry." I hugged her.

She hugged me back, then kissed my cheek. "I can't stay mad at you, any of you."

"Ms. Ines, you remember my girlfriend, now fiancée, Riley?" Sawyer gestured. Riley held up her hand.

"Oh, my! Sawyer, mijo, that is gorgeous. Congratulations." Granny gushed over it. "You lucky girl, Ms. Riley."

"What is this I hear? Sawyer is getting married." Auntie Rita came dancing in. "Let me see the ring!"

She took Riley's hand, examining the ring closely.

"Okay, come and sit. Tell us the story." She pulled Riley to sit on the ottoman then took her seat next to it.

"Well, he asked me to dinner on Friday, said we were going to Mill's Steakhouse."

"Oh, they have good bread," Auntie Rita said.

"They do. I could eat the whole basket by myself." Riley smiled. "Anyway, after we ate, he took my hand and listed all the things he loves about me, then he pulled out the ring. I was in tears, of course, and said yes."

"That's beautiful."

"What a great story. I wish you many happy years."

"Thank you." Riley smiled over at Sawyer. He looked on happily.

"So, Ms. Shayla, how are you holding up?" Auntie Rita asked.

"I'm okay."

"Do you need anything, sweetie?"

"No, they have been really great taking care of me." She looked over at the three of us.

"We're happy to have you."

"And, soon, you'll have a real room." Sawyer smiled.

"I have an awesome room. It is way better than the one I had at home."

"Well, it's going to get better, really soon!" Vee said.

"I know it will," Shayla said, smiling, but I could see tears trying to form in her eyes. This was all a lot to manage, especially with her uncle or step-uncle coming to visit like that.

"Well, are we ready to eat?" Granny asked.

Of course, Sawyer was ready, so we all moved into the dining room. Riley and Shayla helped bring in the food. With that we made small talk as we ate. Afterwards, we played cards, laughing and enjoying simple conversation.

"Thank you so much for a fun night."

"The food was excellent."

"Thank you for having me."

We walked out to Shayla's car to find that all four tires had been cut.

"What the—?"

"I'll call the police," Sawyer said, pulling out his phone.

I turned to my grandmother and aunt, knowing the answer to my question before I asked, but still asking.

"Do y'all have security cameras on the house?"

"No."

"Do any of the neighbors?" I started looking up and down the road. Knowing most of the neighbors since I was a child, I knew that answer was likely no as well, but there were a few new families.

"Um, maybe the Tompkins on the end." Auntie Rita pointed three houses down on the opposite side. "I'll go ask them."

I walked the opposite way looking at each house to see if I saw a camera. None. Why was this block stuck in the 1980s? Worse actually, some were stuck earlier than that. I found one house at the end of the block with a doorbell camera.

I didn't know who lived here. I think they'd moved in when I was in high school or just after that.

I knocked on the door as the bell signaled my arrival.

"Hello? Who are you?" A voice came over the doorbell.

"Hi, I'm Jessica Vasquez. My grandmother and aunt live four houses down, in the white house with the yellow trim."

"Ines's granddaughter, the one with the restaurant?"

"Yes, that's me. I wanted to ask about your camera." I paused. No reply so I continued. "My friend's car was vandalized, and I wanted to see if you had gotten any footage of a suspect?"

The door opened revealing the occupant. He was an older gentleman. Short and frail. His hand grasped tightly to the handle of his cane. He had bright, clear eyes and a wide smile.

"I don't know how to see it, but I can let you try. My grandson set this thing up. I can answer the door, but that's the extent of my knowledge." He chuckled, gesturing for me to come in.

"Okay, just one second, let me tell my family." I yelled down to them, then followed him into his house.

His house was neat and tidy, decorated in a nautical theme with white and navy blues. He had a few tall ship models on display. Then I saw a few pictures of him as a young man dressed in his sailor outfit.

"You were in the Navy?"

"Yes, retired after twenty-four years." He straightened as much as his old body would let him. He came to look at the pictures. "So many good memories."

"And, is this your wife?"

"Yes, my Lydia. Gone two, no three years now. We have two children, Rodger and Laura. Then five grandchildren with a great-great grandchild due any day now."

"Nice."

We continued to his living room where a small desk sat in the corner. It had an old model computer on it with a large monitor.

"Here is that crazy contraption." He pointed to his computer. "I don't use it much, but Allen, that's my grandson, he uses it when he comes. He put all kinds of stuff on it, but I don't know how to use any of it. Though I do enjoy playing solitaire."

"I like that game, too."

I wiggled the mouse, and it came to life. On the screen was a picture of him and his wife with an anniversary cake in front of them. I smiled.

A pop-up then asked for his password.

"Do you have a password for it, Mr. ... umm, oh, I don't know your name. I'm sorry."

"Mitch. Just call me Mitch." He leaned over, pulling a paper from a drawer. "I'll type the password."

He typed it out with his one pointer finger. It was a slow process as he looked back and forth. I simply smiled and waited.

"There you go."

"Thank you."

"I love your alphabet soup, by the way. Oh, and the biscuits. Oh, and your burger. How do you make it so juicy?"

"It's a secret." I pressed my finger to my lips. He chuckled.

"I go there twice a week for lunch."

"Well, let me know next time you are in. I'll come say hi." I smiled at him.

"I will!"

We got back to the business of looking for the camera app. I clicked the icon, and it came to life. I saw he had more than just the doorbell camera connected.

Pushing the button, I rewound to the time we arrived.

"There is her car." I pointed as we drove by, but I couldn't see Granny's house from this view.

The cars coming and going meant nothing without being able to see if they stopped by her car or not. The resolution wasn't very good either, so I couldn't tell who was in the cars.

"Do you recognize any as neighbors?" I asked him.

He named a few. "That one isn't familiar. I do know them and them. Not that one and, umm, don't know that one either."

"Is this block usually this busy?"

"Oh, yes, especially on Sundays. People visiting family. I had mine here earlier today."

Yes, Sundays for us meant family dinner, too. Growing up it was at noon, but now that I work, we do it in the evening.

I flipped through the other camera views to see if any pointed down the street, but they were pointing at mostly his house and yard. That made sense but didn't help me.

"Well, thank you. We called the police. If they need to look at this, would you be okay with that?"

"Of course, yes, anything to help."

"Thank you, Mr. Mitch and it was wonderful to meet you."

"It was so wonderful to meet you, too."

He walked me to the door.

When I got back to Granny's house, I noticed Granny, Auntie Rita, and my friends were sitting on the porch chatting. I also saw that two officers had arrived. One was my friend, Officer Lupe Perez. The other was someone I didn't know. Perhaps a new officer.

They were working on the car. It looked like taking prints from various places.

"Hey, Jess, did you find anything?" Officer Perez asked.

"Not much, but Mr. Mitch is willing to share what he has."

She nodded and made a note.

"This is Officer Bruce Phelps. He just started with us."

"Nice to meet you." I held my hand out. He hesitated to shake it but did. That was strange.

"You're the chef, right?"

"Yes, I own The Crock Pot over on Vine Street and Brush Avenue."

He nodded.

"We called Elias's Tire and Auto," Perez said, as she shifted her weight, giving me a slight smile. Why did she seem awkward? Was it the new partner?

"Thank you."

Elias was an old friend from middle school. He had helped me with tires once when I had my tires slashed. Why did people go for the tires? It was more annoying than sending a message to stop or whatever it was supposed to be. I don't know. If I was mad at someone, my instinct wasn't to go after their car. I just cooked something yummy for myself and moved on.

"We took some pictures, got prints, and we'll go talk to the two neighbors with cameras. Unfortunately, right now, that's all we can do," she said.

"Thanks, Lupe. We appreciate it."

Before they could leave to talk to the neighbors, Elias's Tire and Auto arrived. I was not expecting Elias to be the one to take a Sunday night call, but I also didn't know how his business worked. Maybe he was the only employee.

"Hey, Jess, Sawyer. Congrats, my man! I heard the news. Is this your girl here?"

"Yeah, man, thanks. This is Riley. The future Mrs. Hart."

"Nice to meet you."

"Hey, Genevieve." He turned to Vee. She giggled.

"Nobody calls me that except my mother, and only when I'm in trouble." She pushed a piece of hair behind her ear.

"You look good." He smiled.

"So do you."

"And, I take it this is your car?" He addressed Shayla, but only taking his eyes from Vee for a moment.

"Yes, I don't know who would want to do this. Is it going to be expensive to replace?"

"Nah, you get the friends and family discount." He winked at her.

"Don't worry, Shayla. We got you," Sawyer said, putting his arm around her shoulders. Riley wrapped her arm around Shay's waist.

"Yes, you are like our little sister."

"Thanks, y'all but..."

"No, buts. We got you," Vee added.

"Wow, lots of love here. I feel left out." Elias chuckled. He then turned towards the officer. "Am I good to start my work?"

"Yes, but we will want the tires for evidence," Officer Phelps said.

"Of course."

The officers went to gather any footage from the neighbors. Sawyer stayed with Elias while the rest of us went to the porch. We made small talk with Granny and Aunt Rita. Elias and Sawyer made quick work of the tires, but it was much later than we wanted to get home.

With a promise to follow up if they found anything, the officers left.

We settled with Elias. He and Vee traded phone numbers, then we headed home, which was thankfully uneventful.

Chapter Nine

I smoothed black slacks, wiping a bit of cat hair off of them. I paired it with a cream-colored blouse and a gray cardigan. Today was going to be a tough day. For one, supporting Shayla as she said goodbye to her mother. Then two, being judged by her family and friends as her new guardian.

It was a lot of pressure to be in charge of a teenager, especially one I wasn't related to.

I swiped a little mascara on my eyelashes, then ran a brush through my hair, before jogging down the stairs to see if the others were ready.

Shayla was sitting at the kitchen island scrolling on her phone.

"You ready for this?"

"How does one get ready for the funeral of their murdered parent?" she sarcastically asked, adding an eye roll on the end.

I knew the attitude wasn't pointed towards me. We had already talked about how sucky this whole situation was and that was why she seemed so snarky.

"The same way one prepares to visit their father in prison for birthdays and holidays." I hugged her.

"Yeah, I know you get it." She hugged me back. "At least I will get to see my sisters finally."

Their grandmother was keeping them far away from all of this and that included Shayla, but their therapist had suggested this was the right thing for them to do.

Shayla had called again yesterday to try to talk to her sisters. That's when Lynn told her they would be at the funeral and that she could talk to them there.

"Under my supervision, of course. I don't need you hurting them any more than you have."

Sitting near Shayla while she was on the phone, I had to fight the urge not to snatch her phone so I could tell that woman off. She had no idea the trauma poor Shayla was going through herself. Seeing her sisters would make her feel so much better.

Vee joined us downstairs minutes later.

"Don't you both look nice," she said.

"So do you," Shayla said.

"Are we ready?"

"Sawyer and Riley are still meeting us there, right?" Vee asked.

"That's what he said."

He had recently started staying over at Riley's as he started the process of moving in with her. This weekend, his plan was to finish it up. He said he would get it ready for Shayla and start moving her upstairs.

We headed out to my car, but all looked at Shayla's car, giving it a quick once over. It looked fine. Having been vandalized on Sunday, we were all a bit paranoid and had her parking right in front of our door. We had two security cameras here so it should catch anyone or anything messing with it.

One was pointing directly at the street and the other was aimed at our door, but it got part of the street as well. There were others, but those had the best view of her car.

Driving mostly in silence, we pulled into the Caruso Funeral Home parking lot with ten minutes to spare until the services would start. There were about a dozen or so cars.

"More cars than I thought," Shayla mumbled, her eyes darting around. She mumbled something else I couldn't understand, but it sounded like she was looking for her sisters.

"Are you ready?"

"No, but let's go."

We shuffled inside.

"Ah, Chef Jessica. My hero," Gio Caruso greeted me.

A few months ago, I saved his business and prevented him from being killed. He lost his family, who were the ones trying to kill him, but at least he still had his business and life. For that, he said he would give me a ten percent discount on my funeral needs.

Gosh, I hope that wasn't something I'd need anytime soon.

"Hi, Gio. It is good to see you."

"Are you Shayla?" he asked.

"Yes, sir."

"My deepest condolences for your loss, dear." He squeezed her hands.

"Thank you," she mumbled.

"Shayla!" a little voice yelled out.

"Shay? Where?" another voice yelled.

"Ivy, Dove!" She ran to them, wrapping the two little girls in her arms. All three girls were sobbing and laughing at the same time. It was such a sweet reunion.

She had shown me pictures of them, so I recognized them right away. They looked like lighter versions of her. They were fraternal twins. Dove was a bit taller and a bit heavier. Ivy had strawberry blond hair, while Dove had light, almost white, blond hair.

Watching them greeting their sister was heartwarming. I felt a tug at missing out on this kind of relationship in my life. My brothers were the worst.

I smiled on and looked over at Vee.

"We missed you."

"Mama's dead," Ivy said, whimpering.

"I know. I know. We will be okay, though. We will be okay." She hugged and kissed them.

"Girls, come here," a voice snapped.

We all looked to see an older woman with a pinched frown staring at us. She had long, gray frizzy hair and harsh unblinking eyes. I fought the urge to shiver as a chill crept up my spine.

The little girls clung to their big sister. Ivy kept looking up at her.

"Hi, Grandma Lynn," Shayla finally said.

"Hi, Shayla." Her hesitation on the two syllables of her name said a lot about her dislike. It was like a cavern of hatred. "Girls, I said come here."

"We want to stay with Shayla," Dove whined.

"Now!"

They dropped Shayla's hand and slowly made their way to their grandmother, looking over their shoulders at us.

"Can we sit with her?" Ivy asked.

"Please, oh, please?" Dove begged.

Lynn looked over at us, eyeing Shayla closely.

"Fine, but you stay close to me. I don't know most of these people and I don't want to lose either of you."

The little girls cheered but stayed close to their grandmother.

"This is Jessica and Vee, by the way. They are the people who took me in." Shayla gestured.

"Nice to meet you," I said. Vee simply nodded.

"I'm glad someone took you in," Lynn said. "You own that restaurant?"

"Yes, The Crock Pot."

"Well, umph."

What did that mean? I looked down at Vee. She gave a slight shrug.

We all turned to make our way into the main reception area. There were actually quite a few people in here. I was surprised by that as my impression of Kenna was negative.

"Who are all these people?" I whispered to Shayla.

"I don't know. I recognize a few people, but most of these are strangers to me."

We followed Lynn and the girls to the casket. It was closed but there was a large spray of white and pink roses, carnations, and lilies with a large picture of Kenna in the middle of it.

It was a good picture of her. The few times I met her, she looked like she'd crawled out of the sewer with her dirty, ill-fitting clothing, stringy, greasy hair, and her gaunt face. In this picture, she had color on her cheeks and a smile on her face.

The entire reception room was decorated in the same flowers and there was a table full of family pictures. It was a beautiful set up.

"I didn't know she had dimples," I whispered.

"Yeah, that's where I got mine." Shayla smiled to show me. It was one of the first things I had noticed about her when she did smile. "Ivy has them too."

"Look, Shay, mama was beautiful," Dove said, pulling at her.

"Yes, she was."

"I miss her." Dove started to quietly cry which started Ivy crying. Shayla bent over to hug them.

Lynn Lloyd made an exasperated exhaling sound. I shot her a look.

"What?" she asked.

I lowered my voice. "I think you could have more sympathy. They lost their mother."

"Some mother. She always put them in danger, and that man, ack. He was awful. Ezra was always right about him."

"And, he is now deceased as well, so have some respect."

"Look, little miss chef, I have those two little girls to watch out for now and I don't need some nobody coming over here telling me how to feel, how to act, or how to raise them. I didn't like Kenna and Mikey. And I'm glad they are gone. Regardless how I felt about Kenna, I'm going to do my very best for those girls, but also for my son, their father while he is still in prison."

"Grandma, stop," Ivy whined. "Our mother..."

Her sobs turned to wails of grief. These poor girls.

Shayla picked her up, whispering words of comfort to her. Dove patted her back, shooting their grandmother a dirty look.

"Now, look!" Lynn snapped. "You have upset the girls."

"That was you. Not me. You can't be hateful to their mother, especially today." I really didn't care if she was hateful about Mikey. There was not a soul I knew that was mourning him. Well, maybe his brother.

"And what do you know?"

Before I could answer, Harlow rushed up.

"Look, I don't know what is going on, but you are ruining my sister's service."

"I don't even want to be here!" Lynn blustered.

"Then leave!"

"I don't wanna go," the girls both whined.

"Leave them with me," Shayla said.

"Fat chance. You are as bad as your mother."

"Whoa, whoa. Stop right there, Lynn," Harlow said. "My sister wasn't perfect, far from it, but Shayla is going places. She will be going to Florida in just a few weeks for a huge cooking competition. The same one that Jessica won years ago. Now look at her. Successful business owner and chef. Now I will ask you again to please be respectful or leave, but the girls are staying."

"Fine. Fine." She stomped over to a nearby chair, taking a seat.

"Thank you, Aunt Harlow," Shayla said.

"Did you see the beautiful picture?" Harlow pointed.

"That's how I want to remember her. What about y'all?" She looked down at her sisters.

"Yes."

"Mama." Dove touched the picture gently.

"How are things going with you and Shayla?" Harlow turned to me.

"Good. Very good. She's a perfect roommate."

"She was always a good kid."

There were loud voices outside the reception. Before anyone could react, in strode Jay, Mikey's brother. Hanging on his arm was a woman in skimpy clothes. She was overflowing through the mesh in the top she wore. There were also a few other guys following behind them. They were laughing, pushing each other as they came into the room.

"Oh, I do *not* think so." Harlow marched over to them. "I thought I told you that you weren't welcome here."

"Look, bitch, I ain't here for you. I'm here to support my brother's wife and her girls," Jay snarled, swaying on his feet.

A few men, who I didn't know, stepped closer to Harlow. One put his arm around her. That must be her husband.

"Okay, you came. Now leave," he said. I think it was Darren, but I hadn't yet been introduced officially.

"And who are you?"

"I'm Kenna's brother-in-law and her husband." He pointed to Harlow. "My wife has said you aren't welcome, and so I am saying you aren't welcome."

"Let me just… there… Shay! Hey, Shay! I wanted to tell you about Mikey's funeral."

"Okay, let's go out in the lobby," Shayla said, passing the girls off to Lynn. "I will be right back. Let me deal with him."

She nodded to me, so I followed with Vee on our heels.

"I'm here, Jay, what's up?"

"What is that chick's problem?"

"That *chick* is my aunt and mother's sister. A little kindness goes a long way."

"Whatever. But, hey, Mikey's service is on Monday at three at Pinehurst Memorial Funeral Home."

"So, in Pinehurst?"

"Yes. I know you got school, or whatever, but Mikey ain't got people like this." He gestured towards the room.

"I will try, but like you said, I do have school." Shayla looked over her shoulder. "Now, we thank you for coming, but as a favor to me, please go."

I was so impressed by her strength and authority. She directed these grown, scary people out of here and they listened.

"Okay, I said what I wanted to say." He turned to his friends. "Let's go. Oh, wait? Did you get to talk to the police again?"

"No. Why, did you hear something new?"

"Just Bobo has been saying stuff all over town."

"He confessed?"

"No, no, nothing like that. Just like *he got what he deserved* and *good riddance*, stuff like that."

"Oh."

Jay looked at Vee and I, gave a nod, then whistled for his friends. We watched as they all walked out.

"You okay?" Vee asked her.

"Yeah, but what else can go wrong at this thing?"

"We are here for you."

"Speaking of here, where is Sawyer?" she asked.

As if on cue, in came Sawyer. No Riley with him.

"Hey, sorry that I'm late. Riley got called into work, but I was waiting for her and then well, now I'm late."

"Thanks for coming." Shayla hugged him.

"Did I miss anything?"

"Oh, so much, but we can talk about it later."

We rejoined the people in the reception. Harlow came over to talk to us.

"Thank you for getting rid of them. Ick. They are horrible." Harlow made a fake gagging face. "Oh, Jess, Vee, and Sawyer, right? I can't believe I blanked on your name. Well, anyway, this is my husband, Darren."

"Hi, nice to meet you." We all shook his hand.

"It's nice of y'all to take our little Shayla bear in." He grabbed her, giving her a huge bear hug.

He was a tall man, taller than me and Sawyer. He had an easy smile and fun energy about him. It had me looking at Harlow again. She was also on the taller side, but maybe five foot nine or ten. She was a fast talker and wanted everything just right. No funny business with her.

"Well, we will let you all mingle."

We went to sit near Lynn and the little girls. They both climbed into Shayla's lap, or at least tried to.

"That was really incredible of you. I didn't know you had it in you," Lynn whispered to Shayla.

"It was the right thing to do."

"Look, I'm sorry for being protective of the girls. You can't blame me." Shayla simply nodded her response so Lynn continued. "We can work out something where you can see the girls, okay?"

"I would love that. Thank you so much."

Vee squeezed my hand. It was a good moment after all the drama. Minutes later, the service got started. Thankfully there wasn't any more drama in the day.

Chapter Ten

I came out of my room, ready to head to work and smacked right into a wall of boxes. Today was Sawyer's official move out day.

"Oops." I backed up.

"Whoa! Sorry about that, Jess," Sawyer said, sliding them out of my way. "I thought I'd have it moved before you came out of your room."

"How's it going?" I moved carefully around the boxes.

"Okay, but slower than I thought. Oh, I have a few questions about stuff before you leave."

"Alrighty."

We headed downstairs where he had piles of things all over.

"I didn't even know you had so many things."

"Yeah, I don't think all of it is mine, which is why I have questions." He looked around. "I think we can all agree that most of the kitchen stuff is yours, but what about this?"

He pulled out a huge ceramic beer stein. It had dragons drinking beer carved into it. I loved dragons, but it was definitely not my style.

"Um, I think that's yours."

"Awesome! What about this?" This time, he pulled out a waffle maker. But not just any waffle maker. No. This one made waffles into the shape of his favorite video game characters.

"Oh, that's tough, but I think, no, I know, you can have it."

"Score!" He grinned, turning to Riley. "I am going to make you piles of zombie waffles."

"Oh, boy!" She cheered, but then turned towards me, mouthing *help me*.

I fought the urge to giggle at them.

"Anything else in question?" I asked.

"Not in here, but, oh, oh, what about the painting of the clown riding the dragon in the hall?"

Again, loved dragons, but hate the clowns.

"That's all you."

"Yes! Milo and Jet are coming with us, babe."

"Um, wait. Can we talk about that one?"

"You don't like them?" Sawyer frowned.

"It's not that I don't like them, but I have my place decorated how I like it."

"What about my stuff?" he asked.

I backed out of the room making my way quietly to the front door, waving slowly. Then I stepped out of the house, making my escape from the chaos and what sounded like it was going to be an epic fight. They didn't need me here for that.

Once the door was shut, I made a run for my car. Safe inside, I burst out laughing. I loved him, but he had some interesting things. I looked up at the house as I drove away.

"Good luck, Riley. He's all yours now," I muttered to myself.

Before I could get to the restaurant, my phone rang. I giggled as I hit the button on my car.

"Hello."

"Hey, Jess." Raff's voice filled my car and sent a tingle to my stomach.

"Hey, good morning."

"And, a good morning to you."

"To what do I owe the pleasure of this call?" I laughed to myself. Who was I? I don't think I'd ever uttered that phrase before.

"Just wanted to call before the day got crazy."

"What do you know that I don't?" Had he just jinxed my day?

"Oh, no, sorry, I just meant busy. It's Saturday and I know the restaurant is busy on Saturdays."

An instant relief filled me when I realized his meaning. He was right. Saturdays were busy as far as there would be a lot of people coming through. Weekends meant family time or time with friends. From shopping to sightseeing around town.

And, with it nearly being Christmas time, we had a lot of people from other cities coming to Dashwood for the special boutique and artisan-owned shops with lots of unique gifts. All the shop owners ran specials and sales during this time of year trying to attract the customers.

Plus, there weren't the predictable meal times like during the week, when most people came between eleven and one as they had lunch breaks for work. No, on weekends, it was busy from open to close.

"It makes the day go faster and it's what I signed up for." I laughed.

He chuckled, too. "True, true."

"Well, I'm pulling in to work now. Talk later?"

"Yep, have a good one, Jess."

"You too." I smiled as I headed into work. *What a wonderful start to the day.*

Hours later, as predicted, the day was busy, and I was finding it harder to find the good. As a pretty positive person, my patience was being tested.

Our toilets overflowed in both bathrooms just as we opened for the day. Thankfully, Arlo was able to get the mess cleaned up and Noah got us a plumber out quickly. However, we had to go through lunch without a bathroom for customers.

I'm sure we'd get some bad reviews for that, but it couldn't be helped.

Next, our new dishwasher left the sink running while he ran clean dishes to our stations. At least it was just a matter of cleaning up water. No plumbing issues, but it was a preventable distraction.

"I'm so sorry, Chef. I wasn't thinking," Damon said.

"That's okay. Pay closer attention," I said through a tight smile.

I was a patient person, but even I had my limits, and this day was making it hard not to be one of those yelling chefs. Then, it got worse.

Another new employee dropped two full orders. One was in the kitchen, easy to clean up and move on. However, the other was all over the customer. Thankfully, it was a turkey club sandwich, and not soup. That could have turned into a lawsuit.

Not to mention how busy we were today. We had an hour wait to get seated and a line out the door. It was a good problem to have, but I was working a double today. I was exhausted and ready to crash into bed and I was only just starting the second half of my day.

"Hey, Chef, have you seen Shayla?" Natalie asked.

"I thought she just came in, no?" I could have sworn I'd seen her.

"I thought so, too, but I don't know where she went."

With a slight slowdown of customers, I took it as a chance to take a break. I would be working until close tonight, so I needed to recharge a minute.

I started by walking through the whole kitchen, including the walk-in fridge, freezer, and then the storage area. No Shayla.

"Hm, weird." I know I saw her come in.

I walked towards the office, thinking I could check the cameras, but I heard a noise from the break room, so I headed that way. That's when I saw her weeping softly in the corner, head in her hands.

"Shayla?" I sat next to her, wrapping my arm around her. She let out a soft whimper as she leaned into me.

We stayed like that as I just held her, letting her cry. No words were needed. She was grieving and this was just part of that process.

Eli came into the room. We made eye contact. He held up his hands as he backed out of the room.

After a few minutes, Shayla looked up.

"Sorry, Chef. I just … I got into my head about everything and, well, I couldn't hold it in anymore." She sniffled. "I'll get to work."

She stood, but didn't make a move to leave the room. Tears continued down her face. My heart broke for her. There was a lot going on with her right now.

"Take a few minutes to gather yourself. It's okay."

She collapsed again into full sobs, sitting back down and leaning into me. I pulled her tightly, trying my best to comfort her, but knowing there was nothing I could really do or say to make this better.

Natalie came in while I was rocking Shayla again.

"Oh, sorry." She started to leave but stopped. She came over to us, wrapping her arms around us, too. We all stayed like that for a minute or two, before Natalie said "I can stay for the evening, if you want to go home, Shayla."

Shayla looked up at her, wiping a tear. "Thank you, but no. No, I can do it."

This time she stood, wiped the remaining tears. She plastered on a smile.

"Okay, I got this." She looked at both of us. "Thank you both for the support."

With that she walked out, leaving us there.

"Is she okay?"

"I think so but just has moments." Though I wasn't convinced she was okay. Maybe I should talk to her about taking today off. I would still pay her, of course, so she wouldn't have to worry about that.

Natalie gave a nod and left me sitting in the breakroom. I should have left but my body was exhausted by the day, and no matter what, I couldn't get myself to stand.

"Hey, Jess, what're you doing in here?" Noah said.

"I found Shayla in here."

He looked around. "Um, where is she now?"

"In the kitchen."

"You okay?"

"Tired. No, strike that. I'm exhausted from today." I paused. "And worried about Shayla. She was in here crying."

"My heart hurts for her."

"Mine too."

"Did you offer her to take a day off?"

"No, but Natalie said she would take her shift. Shayla declined the offer and went to work instead."

"Well, she knows what she needs." Noah smiled.

"Do you really think she does? As her temporary guardian, her friend, her boss, shouldn't I advocate for her when she doesn't know what's best for her?"

He paused, mouth slightly open. "Um, you might have a point."

"Yeah." I stood, my muscles screaming. "I'll go talk to her."

When I walked into the kitchen, she was working away plating two slices of pecan pie, throwing them into the pickup window and calling for a runner. Then she turned to add apple pie filling to a pie shell before sliding it into the oven. Unlike some other restaurants, we baked almost all day.

I always hated going for a slice of pie somewhere only to be told they just sold the last piece or didn't have that flavor today.

Next, I watched her grab a scoop, quickly filling a sheet pan with vanilla cookie dough. They went well with our banana pudding.

She was working smoothly and keeping busy, so perhaps that's what she needed. I know it helped me to keep busy.

As I stood there watching her, I felt this overwhelming feeling of joy and pride.

Is this how mothers, aunties, grandmothers felt? Me, the person who never thought I'd have kids was now in this almost mother role to a teenager.

"Chef?" She caught me watching. At home, she called me Jess, but here I was chef.

"I was just … watching you work. You're like a well-oiled machine. Smooth and precise."

"I guess that's good?"

"Yes, very good." I stepped closer for privacy. "You okay?"

"Yeah, I'm better. This will keep my mind and body busy."

"Okay, but if you don't think you can, I'm okay with us just not having a pastry chef tonight. Someone else can plate desserts and we'll just run out at some point."

"No, we can't do that. I can do this. It's in the slow, quiet moments that I remember and have time to miss my mother or think about my sisters."

"Well, I'll be here all night if you need anything."

"Thanks." She smiled then went back to the cookies.

I quickly did the rounds around the entire kitchen, checking in with each employee, then headed to the office. Noah had just left for the day, but I wanted to give a quick shout to Cullen.

"Hey, Cullen."

"Oh, hey, Chef. How's it going?"

"Good, good. I mean today was crazy and I'm not looking forward to my double-shift, but hey, it beats not being busy, right?" I tried to laugh, but today had really kicked my rear.

"Amen to that!"

"Well, just checking in with you."

"All good so far, but I've got your back tonight." He smiled.

Cullen and I had only worked on the same shift a half-dozen times. I normally worked day shift, and he worked the evening shift, but I liked him. He was a great addition to our team. He was smart, caring, and funny. He had golden retriever energy which seemed to draw people to him.

"Oh, before I forget, did you find that car?"

"Unfortunately, not yet. I mean, yes, I found the footage but I'm still reviewing all the video. It is a lot and trying to trace which way it went is taking time. Plus, it's a common sedan so I keep losing it when it passes another like it."

"Yeah, I drive the same make and model."

"So does my mom."

"Well, I really appreciate you trying."

"Of course. Happy to flex these skills, too. Keep them fresh." He winked.

"I better get back to the line."

The evening shift was almost as busy and exciting as the day shift. I was a walking zombie by the time I left for the night. At least being here tonight, I was able to keep an eye on Shayla and her mental health. She kept busy and was genuinely smiling.

"Race ya home!" She giggled when we were leaving that night.

"You're on." But honestly, I was lucky I could remember how to drive and just followed her without trying to actually race.

When we got home, she parked by the front door again and I pulled in behind her. We headed in and the house felt different.

"Wow, I didn't think it would be this noticeable to have Sawyer gone," she said.

"Yeah, I didn't either." I looked around. "Oh, but, hey, it's your last night in the spare room."

"Yes, that will be different." She smiled.

"Well, good night."

"Night, Jess. Oh, and thanks for everything. It really means a lot."

I smiled as I dragged myself to bed. I was so glad I had the ability to help her.

Chapter Eleven

"I like this one." Shayla picked up the color palette. She pointed to a grayish-blue color. "It's called silver waves."

"That's pretty. It will match your bedspread well," Vee said, as she pulled up another one. "Do you want any other colors? Like to do stripes or a design? Because this one would match nicely."

"It's nice, but no, that will be too busy for me. I like calm. Plus, I can add artwork." She got excited. "Oh, oh, we can go to the comic book store. Mr. Monte said he had some new things coming in."

While they shopped, I was holding onto the cart like my life depended on it. After working all day yesterday, from opening until closing, I was just trying to keep my eyes open.

Sawyer had finished his move out yesterday while I was at work, and before we moved Shayla to his room, we were going to clean and paint.

That was the great thing about our landlord, he let us do what we wanted as long as it was value added and didn't damage the property. Painting was fine.

"I paint between all my tenants anyway, so go for it," Lamar had told us when we signed.

That was years ago, and we hadn't left yet. Unless Vee and I met and married people, we would likely live together until we died. At least, I had no plans to move away from her any time soon, if ever.

I yawned as they went to have the paint mixed. There was definitely a nap in my future, especially since we weren't going to Sunday dinner at my grandmother's. This week it was my Uncle Sully, Aunt Gina, and their two awful children, Nova and Junior. They were my cousins, and while I loved them, because they were family, I didn't like them very much.

Vee put some paint rollers in the cart and Shayla grabbed the now mixed paint cans.

"You ready?"

"Hm? Oh, yeah," I mumbled.

I shuffled behind them to the register. The cashier smiled brightly.

"Hey, aren't you Chef Jessica? From the television shows?"

I plastered on my television smile as I summoned some energy. "Yes, that's me."

"Oh, I knew it." She looked around, and seeing the person she was looking for, she yelled to him. "Steve, hey, Steve… Look who it is? That chef we like from all those food shows."

A guy, I assume named Steve, turned and came over, a huge smile on his face.

"Wow, it is. Would it be weird if I asked for your autograph?" he asked, pulling out a small notepad from his shirt pocket.

"Sure. Happy to."

I took the pen and notepad Steve held out, then wrote a quick note of well wishes and signed it. When I passed it back, the cashier thrust a scrap of receipt tape and a pen at me.

"Me too!"

I looked at her name tag. "Beth?"

"Yep, that's me. Bethany, but I go by Beth. My mother wanted Bethany, but my father said it was too fancy for a little girl, so Beth is what I have always gone by. Only my mother calls me Bethany." She stopped, grabbing her face. "Oh, gosh, I'm rambling. I'm so nervous. I mean, it's you! I have never met a celebrity before."

Vee and Shayla giggled together as they watched. It was probably a bit humorous and not something I dealt with often. I'd never felt like a celebrity.

"There you go." I handed it back. She read it, then smiled.

"Thank you so much." She kept staring. Steve cleared his throat. "Oh, yes, sorry, sorry. Just a big fan."

She began ringing up the items, making small talk as she did, then Vee paid.

"An early birthday present," Vee said when Shayla tried to argue.

"Thanks, Vee."

Beth waved as we left. "Come again!"

"Do we go to the comic book store now, or another day?" Vee asked as she started the car.

"I think another day. It's going to take time to paint the room, plus I need to finish cleaning it."

"Okay, then home we go."

I yawned as I daydreamed about my warm bed and the incoming nap. I leaned my head back on the seat rest and settled down in the back seat, thinking I might get a quick snooze on the way home.

But before we could even leave the parking lot, a large man stepped in front of the car. He pointed at Shayla.

"Oh, crap, that's Hawk."

"Who's Hawk?" Vee and I asked.

"Shay, roll down the window," he said.

"I'll tell y'all later. Hey Hawk," she said as soon as her window was open.

"Hey, baby girl." My body tensed at his choice of greeting and an icy chill ran through me. It was creepy. He continued "I was sorry to hear about your mom and Mikey. You okay?"

"Yeah, I'm okay." She squirmed in her seat.

"I'm going to miss my boy, man." He rubbed his stubbled face. "Any ideas on who?"

"No, none. You?"

"Could be a lot of folks, honestly." He looked at Vee and I, then back at me. "Hey, you that chef?"

"Yeah, that's me."

"Cool. You the one that gave baby girl here a job?"

I wanted to correct him and say she earned it, worked hard for it, and wasn't given anything. I mean, she needed to be recognized for her dedication and work ethic, not thought of as someone who was just given something. Studying him, I knew it wouldn't matter, so I kept it short.

"She works hard."

"Cool. Welp, baby girl, call me if you need anything. Your father was like a brother to me."

"Stepfather," she corrected.

"Right, right. Whatever. Mikey will be missed." He tapped the window before backing away.

She closed it as quickly as it would go up. "Go. Now before he comes back."

Vee stepped on the gas and got us out of the parking lot and down the road before he could even give us a second glance.

"What was that about?" I asked, leaning forward from the back seat.

"Okay, so I'm sure you got the gist. A friend of Jay and Mikey's since they were children. He was one of the guys that was always around. He creeps me out."

"Yeah, me too."

"Yep, same."

"Other than that, nothing special about him. Just that creepy vibe about him, like you just know not to be alone with him." She shuddered. "I hope I never see him again."

"I get that."

"Yes, hope not."

As we drove, we all looked around to make sure we weren't being followed. Thankfully, we made it home without any issue.

We unloaded the paint and supplies. Dropping everything in Shayla's new room, I glanced around. This had been Sawyer's room since we moved in. At first, we all thought it would just be a year or two, but as the years ticked by, it got to the point we thought it would be forever.

Now it was just me and Vee left of the original three.

"So, weird to think he is gone after all these years together," I said.

"Yeah, but he and Riley are happy, and we get to go to a fun, fancy wedding!"

"You think it will be fancy?" I asked.

"All weddings are fancy, even the informal and simple ones." Vee chuckled. "We get to dress up, get our hair done, and nails painted up. I can't wait."

"You know, I can paint your nails. I'm really good at it, even designs," Shayla offered. "I watch a lot of Tik Tok vids."

"Okay, maybe after we get this room done," Vee said.

"Do y'all need help? Or can I nap?"

"Nap, for sure. We can manage this," Vee said.

"Yes, you worked hard the last two days, especially yesterday. Oy!" Shayla said.

"Yeah, yesterday was awful." I chuckled. "Thanks. If y'all are still at it when I get up, I'll jump in."

"Sounds like a plan."

"And, we'll try to keep the noise down."

Lulu was in my bed when I climbed into it. I scratched her around the ears and under her chin. She yawned and curled up in a tighter ball. Stretching once, I rolled to my side and remembered nothing after that as I fell into a deep sleep that lasted for a few hours.

I sat up and looked around for Lulu. She was gone.

Such a cat, I thought as I swung my legs over the bed. I ran to the bathroom then went to search for my friends.

I didn't find them in Sawyer's old room, now Shayla's, but they had finished all the cleaning and much of the painting. The color looked really good. Then I heard voices downstairs, so I followed them to the office.

"Hey, y'all. The room looks good."

"Thanks! We got a lot done but wanted a break."

"What are y'all doing in here?"

"She painted my nails. Aren't they gorgeous?" Vee wiggled her fingers in my direction.

I grabbed her hand to check them out. Shayla had drawn geometric designs on each finger. "These are great. You did the design?"

"Yep. I used to practice on my sisters. It kept them quiet and still."

"Why?" Vee asked.

"When mom and Mikey would be … ya know, drinking and stuff, they would sometimes get violent. It would be best if I kept the girls away from them. Painting their fingers and toes meant they had to sit still while it dried."

"I'm sorry," I said. That made me sad for them all, but it explained her close relationship and wanting to protect her little sisters. "I'm not as good as you at the nails, but I can paint yours."

"Really? I'd love that."

She pulled out an organizer loaded with various colors of polish and pen type paints. We selected a base color, and I started.

"We were also trying to figure this thing out," Vee said, gesturing to the clue board.

"Any luck?" I looked at the board. They had added Hawk's name but there wasn't much else to say. He was creepy, but he seemed to be grieving the loss of his friend, just as much as others. "Thoughts on Hawk?"

"He just creeps me out, so I feel like he deserves a place as a suspect. No other reason," Shayla said. "Honestly, I doubt he did it. He's too lazy."

"We need to start finding some real clues or we will never solve this."

"Maybe call Detective Upton to see what he knows," Vee suggested, then she giggled. "Or ask Rafferty?"

"I am not asking Raff. It feels like a conflict of interest or whatever you want to call it."

"But, it's the perfect in to finding out stuff," Vee said.

"I know, but I just don't want to use him for information. I know what that feels like."

"Todd," they both said in unison.

"Yeah, Todd. But maybe I will call Detective Upton tomorrow. I hate to call him on a Sunday." I painted Shayla's last nail. "There. What do you think?"

"They look great. Thanks!" She smiled. "By the way, once I get my room upstairs together, I was wondering if I could have a few friends over for a sleepover."

"Oh, of course. Sleepovers are fun."

"I wouldn't know. I've never had one."

"Well, we are going to fix that!" I looked over at Vee.

"Heck, yeah, we are. We'll have movies, junk food, and spa treatments. What do you think?"

Shayla laughed. "Yeah, that sounds fun. Thanks."

"Spicy Fig for dinner?" Vee asked.

"Yes, I love that place."

"I haven't been yet, but I keep hearing great things. A kid in my class, his family owns it," Shayla said.

"Nice. Okay, are y'all ready?" I asked.

"Yep."

"Let's go."

We threw on shoes and headed out. This place was fairly new. It opened about a month or so ago. It was owned by a Lebanese family. The owner and chef, Samir Saad had been so sweet the last time I was there, but his oldest son, Anwar was not as nice.

He seemed short tempered as he snapped at staff and was gruff with customers. The food was amazing though, which almost made up for Anwar's attitude.

The last time I'd been there, Samir and I had a wonderful conversation.

"Hey, Chef Jessica. Welcome, welcome," he said.

"Hello, Chef Samir."

"Ah, I'm not a chef, like you're a chef. I just own a restaurant."

"They are your recipes, and you have trained your staff to cook them. I stand by the title."

"You are too sweet."

"So, how are things?" I knew how hard things could be for a new restaurant. I had just struck the market at the right time. Though in the first few months, I wasn't sure if I would and then like the clouds parting after a storm, I was good.

"Oh, a little rough." He looked around. "Anwar is trying but has entered in some crazy business deal with the food vendor and our equipment is leased."

"Leased?"

"Yes, have you ever heard of such a thing? If we don't make one payment, someone will come take it back."

That had me worried about him and his business, so any time I could give him business, I was going to. I also recommended his place to anyone who wanted a new place.

During this visit, I wanted to try more things on their menu. Maybe the lamb skewers with saffron rice with a side of their tomato and cucumber salad.

Chapter Twelve

It wasn't even nine a.m., and I could tell it was going to be one of those Murphy's Law days, where if it could go wrong, it would. I was just waiting on the next crazy thing to happen.

It was like there was a full moon the past week. Why had it been so insane?

We had five people out sick with either the flu or a cold. One of those people was Noah, which meant I had to be the manager for the day. Another was Hannah, which meant I had to be the chef as well.

Gotta love cold and flu season. I thought, as I pulled out my cell phone so I could call Cullen.

"Hello?" His sleepy voice answered.

"Cullen?"

"Yeah? Oh, hey, Jess or, um, Chef."

"Yes, sorry to wake you."

"It's okay. What's up?"

"Are you able to come in a little earlier today? Noah and Hannah are both out sick."

"Which means you have to be the manager and the chef today." Through the phone, I could hear him moving around. "Yeah, I can come in early, but I have an appointment at 10:30. Is noon okay?"

"Yeah, that will help." I can survive until then, I think. "Thank you so much."

The backdoor bell rang. I checked the camera. It was our food vendor, so I hung up with Cullen and went to let Lorenzo in.

"Hey, Lorenzo."

"Hey, Chef." He pushed in his dolly with boxes. "This is your chicken."

"Okay." I grabbed our order sheet, so I could start checking things off. My mind was on all the prep I had to do and that none of my employees had arrived yet. "Wait, all six of these boxes are chicken?"

"Yes. Six chickens." He dropped them at our freezer then started back for the rest.

I followed him. "We ordered four boxes."

"Um, are you sure?"

"I have it right here. This is what Noah put in. He always prints it out."

Lorenzo grabbed his sheet. "Six, right here."

"Well, bleep." I looked at our sheet closer. It was the right date, but why the mix up? Because that's just life right now. "I guess that's fine. We'll definitely use it."

"Great. I'll bring in the rest."

Nothing between the two sheets matched, so I just made notes next to each item. This way I could keep things on track and have a record of what we got. I needed to get on with the day and this was just slowing me down.

"We square, Chef?" Lorenzo asked after unloading the last box.

"Honestly, I don't know. Nothing matches and without being able to confirm with Noah, I'm just going to take it, and we'll figure it out."

"Sorry." He turned to leave. "Good luck, Chef."

The phone rang and it was another employee calling out sick. I tried not to cry in frustration, but I just wished them well and wondered who else I could call in.

June was out of town but would be back to work tomorrow. Parker would be in tonight, I hoped, so for executive chefs, that was it. I didn't have any line cooks ready to step up, but I could double up on them and my prep cooks which would at least help a little bit.

I started calling every employee who was not sick or already scheduled. I managed to get an extra two employees, but they were a runner and a server. Didn't matter, I needed a few warm bodies to give the illusion of more people and if I needed someone to grab something, mix something, or run food, they would be here.

Employees started showing up. I put them to work unloading the food order while I made soups and prepped what I could. My newest line cook, Eli came in and I had him and our prep cook, Justin get all the stations set up.

We were still getting prepped when the first customers showed up, but we would keep working and faking our way through service. The first hour was a blur, but we were doing it. Less organized than normal, but we had only one customer complaint so far, which felt like a miracle.

I glanced at the time. It was almost time for Cullen to be here any second which would help me out a lot, as I could simply focus on the cooking and managing the kitchen.

"Runner!" I threw the plates into the pickup window.

Another new employee, Ian came over, grabbing the plates and turning to leave, he dropped them on the floor with a loud crash. He was the king of dropping plates. Maybe I would talk to Noah and Cullen about letting him go.

He flinched and slowly turned to look at me.

"Ohmygosh. Sorry, Chef!" He started cleaning without hesitation.

That gave me pause on the thoughts of firing him, but he dropped food on a customer the other day and seemed to lose at least one order each day. I'd have to think about it.

Sighing, I had already started working on the next order but now I had to back track. I held my temper, as best I could. My biggest fear had always been giving into anger.

It was a childhood trauma from my dad going to prison for murder. Turns out, the murder had nothing to do with my father's temper. He had been protecting me. In the fight, the other man was shot.

Still, I had lived most of my life this way. Plus, I didn't think it was a bad way to live.

"That's okay, Ian. Just get it cleaned up." I looked over at Eli.

He was swamped, so he couldn't back me up, at least not yet. When Hannah was in that position, she and I had a rhythm where we could back each other up, even at moments like this. Eli and I would get there, I hoped.

The last few days had been so crazy. It was like the past months of smooth sailing had been a fluke and chaos was now how we worked.

The clock hit three and the evening shift started to come in. They only had three people out sick, so they should be in better shape. When Parker came in, I stayed another hour to help get the place cleaned and caught up with soups, restocked the various stations, and ensured he was in a good position for the evening.

"Thanks, Chef. Sorry things were rough today."

"It happens."

I headed to the office so I could talk to Cullen. He wasn't in there, so I went out to the dining room. I found him checking on the Ladies' Book Club that came in this afternoon. They came in once a month at two to meet.

I walked over to greet them. They all got so animated.

"Chef!"

"Chef Jessica, everything was wonderful."

"Oh, the potato leek soup today was delicious."

"Thank you, ladies. I'm so glad to hear you enjoyed yourselves," I said, smiling at them. "Good book this month?"

They all started talking over each other. I could only make out a few replies.

"Yes, wonderful story."

"It was okay."

"My favorite this year."

I tried to reply to all those I heard, but then I needed to get back to work.

"Well, I will let you get back to it." I nodded to Cullen, so he knew I wanted to talk to him.

He said his goodbyes to the group and followed me to the kitchen.

"Thanks so much for coming in early. I will make it up to you."

"Don't worry about it. It was busy."

"And you saw my notes about our food order today?"

"Yeah, I tried to go through it to see what happened, but I kept getting interrupted. I will go through it better tonight."

"Did you find anything else with the security footage with the car that was following Shayla?"

"Yeah, I tracked it through the city, but it went into the camo zone, and I lost it." He dug in his backpack. "I printed a few screenshots for you though. I know we already talked about how this is like so many cars, but just in case."

"Thanks." I took the pictures. "What's the camo zone?"

"It is the part of town where the cameras don't work, or they don't have them. It is the area where Shayla lives."

"The whole neighborhood over there?" How can a whole neighborhood be a blacked-out zone? That seemed so strange in this day and age. But knowing that area, it shouldn't surprise me at all. It was the roughest part of town.

"Yep, and not many residents have them either. I tried accessing the few cameras that were there and never saw this car again." He paused. "I then watched the cameras on the days since, nothing. Nada. Zip."

"It just disappeared?"

"Yep. Sorry, Chef, but that's why it took me a few days to get you all the information."

"It's not your fault, but it definitely makes me feel uneasy."

I thought about Shayla. She was supposed to go visit her sisters tonight after school. The plan was for her to eat dinner there. I sure hoped she was safe, my new internal mom voice thought

"Well, why don't you head home? We got this from here. You had a rough day. Have some wine, put your feet up." He smiled.

"Thanks." I grabbed my stuff and started to walk out. "Oh, and thanks for this." I still held the printouts of the car.

With that I headed home. The plan was to shower and then dive headfirst onto my bed, at least for a short nap.

Vee got home while I was face down in bed, but I wasn't asleep. I heard her pause at my door.

"I'm awake," I mumbled into my pillow.

"You okay?"

I rolled over. "Yeah, busy day."

"I brought us dinner."

"Yeah?" I sat up. "What did you get?"

"Sushi 73."

"Love you!"

We headed downstairs together.

"It's weird not having Sawyer here."

"He has only been gone a few nights," I said.

"I know, but now I drive to work alone and home alone. We have been going to work together for nearly fifteen years."

"Aw, I'm sorry. I hadn't thought of that."

"Yeah, it's going to take some getting used to, but at least he isn't singing all the wrong words to the songs anymore."

"Ha, yeah. He doesn't know any of them."

"No, he does not."

We laughed as we began digging through the bag of food. She'd gotten me a poki bowl with the spicy tuna and extra avocado, just how I like it. She got their ramen.

"I got us each a couple of egg rolls too, just because."

"Yum! Should we eat here or the living room?"

"Living room. It's closer to the TV."

We laughed and took our food into the other room, each sinking into our favorite spot. We ate, chatted, and watched television.

"I talked to Cullen briefly today. He finished reviewing that security footage, but it didn't get us anything. Well, I have screenshots of the car, but no idea who it belongs to. Plus, he said he lost it in the camo zone as he called it."

"Camo zone. A place without cameras?" she asked.

"Yeah, how'd you know?"

"Context."

"I had a rough day. That part of my brain isn't working."

"It does sound rough, but you survived."

"Barely. I am going to sleep like the dead tonight."

"So, back to the car, did he find anything else?"

"Nah, nothing."

The front door opened. Shayla came shuffling in. Lulu came out of nowhere running to her, rubbing on her legs and meowing wildly. Shayla scooped her up and joined us in the living room.

My cat was such a traitor, but honestly, I was glad she loved Shayla.

"Hey, I thought you would be out a little later," Vee said.

"No, the girls needed to go to bed early. Plus, Lynn was being … well, her wonderful self." She made a gagging sound. "She hates me. Always has for no reason."

"Did she say anything specific?"

"No, just made little comments. I think because she hated my mother so much, and I look so much like my mother, at least when she was younger. Honestly, her son, Ezra is no winner. You know he is in prison, right?"

"Yeah, didn't you say he was in Milton County?" I asked.

"Yes."

"That's where my dad is. I wonder if they know each other."

She shrugged. "Maybe. It's a small place, right?"

"Not too small. I think there are 3,000 people in that one. It is one of the larger ones in the state."

"Wow, I didn't know it was that large. We used to go when the girls were babies. Ezra and mom were still kinda dating. I think she broke up with him not long after, then met Mikey about a year later."

"I think the way they manage visitors makes it seem small and intimate. Almost makes you forget you're in a prison. Almost."

I thought of the many visits I have had over the years. I will have the annual Thanksgiving one soon. It would be the first holiday since dad and I cleared the air. It would likely still feel wrong, but I was looking forward to it a little bit.

"How were the girls?" Vee asked, changing the subject. She gave me a small smile, knowing it was hard to think of my father in prison even now.

"They were so happy to see me. They showed me their room with their new clothes and toys. They have a dog there. It is a yappy little thing, but he seemed to like the girls."

"I'm glad you finally got some time with them," I said.

"Lynn said something that has been on my mind ever since. If she would have said it only once, I wouldn't have thought much of it, but she said Ezra is happy they are gone."

"From what you said about his hatred for your mom and Mikey, yeah I bet he is."

"Yeah, but, darn, I wish I could remember exactly *how* she said it. It is just nagging on me," she said.

"Should we put Ezra on the board?" Vee asked with a slight giggle in her voice. She always got ridiculously excited about the murder board.

"Yes!"

"Oh, wait, I should get the pictures of that car and put it on the murder board, too," I said.

"What car?" Shayla asked.

"The one that followed you. Cullen was able to get a couple of screen grabs of it, but unfortunately, no other information and lost it close to your neighborhood."

"Well, that sucks."

We added those two things to the board, then stood back and looked at it. It still wasn't much, but anything at this point.

"Did you get to talk to Detective Upton today?" Shayla asked.

"No. We had a really crazy day at the restaurant and then it just slipped my mind. I'll try to call him tomorrow."

June was going to work the day shift, and Parker would work the evening shift, then I hoped by Wednesday, Hannah would be better so she could work the day shift. I wanted to start enjoying more time off. Though off is a relative term. I planned to test recipes and do more managing, especially with all these new employees, like the butter finger kid, Ian.

"We are not going to solve this tonight," Vee said

"No, we are not."

We turned and went to watch television and gossip until bed. I was glad that today was finally over, and I could sleep. We all made our way upstairs.

"Hey, this is the first time you'll be sleeping in your new room," Vee said when we reached the second floor.

It was supposed to be last night, but the paint fumes had been too much, so she slept one more night in her old room.

"Yes, I'm excited!" Shayla grinned.

We said our good nights. I climbed into bed with the nagging thoughts about Ezra, Bobo the drug dealer, Hawk, and also Grandma Lynn. Not a one of them really stood out yet as a suspect, well maybe Bobo since Jay said Mikey owed him money.

If they owed Bobo money, was it possible he left them the note? Maybe to say I warned you to pay, but now I'm coming for you and my money. Who knows?

I never understood killing over owed money though, because once the person was dead, you'd never get your money back. But I guess it would stop him from using more and owing even more money. That was the last thought as I drifted off to sleep.

Chapter Thirteen

I slept until nearly 10 am,waking up to Lulu standing on my chest. Not sure why I slept so long today. I hope I wasn't getting sick like everyone else at work.

"Good morning, Lulu."

She meowed.

"Are you sad that Shayla went to school, and you're stuck here with me?"

She meowed.

"Fine. I will let you in Shayla's room." I got up and walked to Shayla's new room, opening the door. Lulu twitched her tail at me as she walked in. "You're welcome."

I walked away chuckling. Cats were so funny.

After I went to the bathroom and washed up, I headed downstairs for coffee. Checking my phone, I needed to call Detective Upton. I had a text from Rafferty wishing me a good morning. Even though I knew he would be working, I sent him a text.

I loved that he sent me a good morning text each and every morning. It put a smile on my face.

He replied: **Glad you got to sleep in. Dinner soon?**

Me: **Yes! Definitely.**

I had been working so much lately; we hadn't gotten to go on a second date.

R: **It's a date. I'll call you soon.**

Me: **K**

My coffee was ready, so I grabbed it and went to sit at our kitchen island. I pulled up Detective Upton's number, then hit the call button. I had no idea yet what I was going to say or ask. It just felt like I needed to know what he knew.

"Hello, Jess," he said when he answered.

"Hey, Detective."

"So, I assume you want an update on Kenna and Mikey's murder case."

"I do."

"I don't have anything."

"Nothing?"

"We picked up Bobo, but he was in Florida at the time of the murder and has proof."

"He was the only lead?"

"Unfortunately, at this time yes, except Shayla." When I didn't acknowledge his comment, he continued. "We couldn't get any prints from the scene, other than the family's. There were no cameras in the immediate area and the closest we could get security footage to her house was in a high traffic area. It could have been anyone."

"Did you ever find the car that had followed Shayla?"

"Another dead end."

Cullen hadn't been able to find much from it either, so I wasn't surprised, just disappointed. I had hoped that they had access to better technology or information.

"And her tires?"

"They are still processing the prints, but it isn't looking good. Someone is trying to send a message for sure."

"What is the message? Is she in danger?"

"I don't think so or they would have done something by now."

"How can you be sure? I have a responsibility to keep her safe."

"If I thought either of you were in trouble, I would have a patrol set up." He paused. "I might do that actually, just to be safe."

Maybe Kyle Rafferty could be the extra patrol, then maybe I'd get to see him more.

"Thanks. What can I do?"

"Nothing."

"I have to do something. I can't just sit back and let this go unsolved." I felt frustrated tears forming.

"Jess, I know you want to help, to solve this, but the most important thing you can do now is take care of Shayla. She has no one else."

I wanted to argue that she had her Aunt Harlow, but honestly, Harlow wasn't that involved. She also had her sisters, but they weren't old enough to be of much support. No, he was right, Vee and I were the only ones she had.

"You're right. But I just wish I could do more."

"I know." He paused. "Do you have any ideas on a new suspect?"

I thought for a moment. I had one idea, but I didn't want to share it with him. Though, maybe I'd get a little information.

"Not really, but question, what do you know about Ezra Lloyd?"

"Ezra Lloyd? As in Ivy and Dove's father and Lynn Lloyd's son?"

"Yes. I know he's in prison, but I was just curious about him."

I could almost hear his gears turning. I didn't want him to blow up my plan, which was to talk to my father about Ezra.

"Are you thinking he might have hired, or maybe ordered, someone to kill them?"

"No, but *now* I am." Okay, I had been thinking that, but I didn't want him to know. I hoped to ask my father about it.

"Oh, well, don't start thinking it now. We will solve this. I promise I am doing what I can."

Okay, crisis averted, I hoped. I didn't want him talking to anyone at the prison before I got a chance to talk to people about him. I should have kept my mouth shut on Ezra.

"I know. I just wanted to touch base. Is there anything I *can* do?" I asked.

"Nothing. Nothing at all. Just let me do my job."

"Of course. How is my little buddy?" His son, Aiden, was probably my biggest little fan. He was nearly three years old and from what Brooke, Detective Upton's wife had told me, Aiden liked to play chef.

"He's good. We just bought him a larger kitchen set. He is always talking about his chef friend."

"I love that. Well, I will let you get to work. Thank you."

After we hung up, I just stood there. I didn't know what to do. There wasn't much I could do right now.

"Tomorrow," I said.

Tomorrow is the visit with my father, and I will ask him about Ezra Lloyd. Dad had been in prison for thirty years and would be there for the rest of his life, so he knew everyone. I just hoped that I would get a chance to talk to him, because Granny Ines and Auntie Rita would also be going with me. It would be our Thanksgiving visit, even though Thanksgiving wasn't until next week.

Unfortunately for me, or fortunately depending on how you thought of it, I had decided to have the restaurant open for Thanksgiving and would be working. Though I had a plan that I hoped would work to make it special for everyone.

We had taken reservations so we could plan, though we would take walk-ins if we had space. The reservations had filled up quickly and we were booked. We had a special menu planned which Cullen was toting online to get the buzz going.

Visitors can bring baked goods to the prison only during this special time, from now until the end of the year.

My dad had requested blondies and my oatmeal cookies with nuts and raisins. I took them last year and he enjoyed them a lot.

That's how I spent the next few hours of my day, baking. I wasn't much of a baker, but both of these were simple recipes, so it wasn't a problem. I made extra so I could share. I'd give some to Granny, Auntie Rita, and I would keep some here for us. Plus, I would add a tray of them to the shared table for others.

Satisfied with the results of my baking, I packaged everything into containers. One for Granny and Auntie Rita, one for dad, then one for the shared table.

I ended up not saving any for us here, in favor of sharing what I made. We had Shayla who could bake circles around me.

With that small task done, I got to the business of relaxing for the day.

Early afternoon, I got a text from Rafferty.

R: **Dinner tonight?**

I had to think about that. It would leave Vee on her own because Shayla had to work. Vee was a big girl and could be home alone for one night, but I would still have a little guilt.

Me: **Sounds good**

R: **Pick you up at 6**

Me: **See you then**

As I ran up the stairs to figure out what to wear, I let out a giggle. Lulu came from out of nowhere to run upstairs with me. She launched onto the bed with a loud meow in my direction.

"Are you happy for me?"

Meow, she said.

"Well, I think you would like him. I'll let you meet him soon." I petted her head before turning to flip through my clothes.

I picked out a thick gray sweater and red leggings. My black ankle boots would work and a long silver multiple chain necklace. Laying it out on the bed gave me a chance to look at it all together.

"Yep, perfect."

Lulu meowed as she smelled it and then settled onto the sweater.

"Oh, no, no, no. I don't need your fur on here." I shooed her off and then hung the clothes back up.

I sent Vee a quick text to let her know. She was working but sometimes could check her phone if it was slow.

Me: **Do you want me to make something for your dinner?**

V: **No, I'll be fine. I'm so excited for you.**

Me: **Thanks.**

V: **Oh, customer. Later**

I smiled at the phone. Tonight was going to be a good night for sure.

Chapter Fourteen

Last night had been fun with Rafferty. We went to Pins Bowling Alley for pizza and a few games of bowling. It was perfect.

We both actively kept it off of the topic of the murder, but I know for me, it was on the tip of my tongue to ask questions. I could hear Upton's words in my head.

Stay out of it, Jess.

We ended with a kiss good night. It was amazing.

Now it was time for the drive to visit dad. I loaded up all the goodies and headed out to pick up Granny and Auntie Rita.

I pulled up at the curb in front of Granny's house. Auntie Rita opened the door yelling they would be just a minute. I didn't wait, instead, I hopped out so I could give them the cookies and blondies I had saved especially for the two of them.

"I brought these for you," I said, setting them down in the kitchen.

"Oh, yum. Thanks," Auntie Rita said, peeking into the container and snatching an oatmeal cookie out. "These are the best."

"We have some extras for you and the girls, too," Granny said, pointing to a foil wrapped tray. "You can get them once we get back."

"Sounds good. What can I help carry?"

She handed me a tray of cookies.

"Polvorones and chocolate crinkle cookies."

Her *polvorones rosas,* which are a Mexican sugar cookie, were famous, at least with our family and friends. They are brightly colored circles of love and one of my dad's favorites from his childhood.

"I'll put these in the trunk with mine."

"Great."

Once we were loaded up, I put the car in drive, and we took off. The drive normally took me two hours, but with my granny and aunt, it would likely take me two and half hours. That was fine. We had all day and plenty of time to get there.

"So, what's good with you, Jessie?" Auntie Rita asked from the back seat.

"Oh, just getting ready for next week."

I left out the crazy stuff and how much I'd been working lately. I was so thankful that Hannah was back to normal today. She was able to work her shift, so I didn't miss this visit with my dad.

Next week we were hosting a special Thanksgiving meal at the restaurant. I had asked all staff to help in creating this menu, asking them each what their favorite dish was, then we all worked to put together a menu from the list. It was a fun process, and everyone felt some ownership.

One of my mentors had always done family dinners with his staff, especially for holidays. I wanted to do that, but I hadn't done it yet. This, at least in my mind, was a way to honor my chefs and staff with an almost family dinner like day.

With that in mind, we had given their family and special friends first right to the reservations, then once everyone had theirs, we opened it to the public. The public filled in the rest of the spots, and we had a waitlist.

We were heavily advertising this Thanksgiving event, so hopefully nobody was surprised when they couldn't just walk in and eat.

"We can't wait. We have a reservation at noon," Granny said. "The menu sounds wonderful."

"I love corn casserole and cranberry salad," Auntie Rita said.

"It's going to be a great menu for sure."

"Everyone at church and in our Bible study group is talking about it," Auntie Rita said. "So many couldn't get reservations, so they are jealous." She giggled.

"I wish I could feed everyone."

"Well, I hate to change the subject." That wasn't true. She loved it. "But, Ms. Crime Fighting Chef, are you helping with Shayla's case?" Granny Ines asked. Her voice and eyes were stern, like when I'd get caught stealing a cookie or brought home a bad report card.

"Um, yes, of course. I know she didn't do it." The police knew too, but they still hadn't completely ruled her out.

"Good. I know you will do your best by that girl. I assume you're going to ask your father about Ezra Lloyd and about Mikey's time in Milton County."

I shouldn't be surprised that Granny was plugged in to all the gossip about town. She knew everyone and spent a lot of time with the other ladies. All they did was gossip.

"Mikey was in Milton County, too?"

Shayla had given me bits and pieces, but I felt like there were still parts I didn't know.

"Yeah, for a few years right before Kenna met him. Your father had at least one run in with him."

"I did not know that."

Now I had two people to ask him about. Could there be any connection from someone he knew either while in or who was also released? Would my dad even know about Mikey's life outside of prison?

After two pit stops, we finally made it. I had anticipated the amount of time it would take us to get here and had planned accordingly. We arrived with roughly fifteen minutes to spare. It gave us ample time to get checked in and settled in the visitor room.

"Hey, Ms. Ines, Ms. Rita, and oh, Jess. Hi." Officer Luna Pena greeted us when we went to sign in.

"Hi, Officer Pena."

"Hi, Luna. How's your mama?"

"She's well, Ms. Ines. Thanks for asking."

"I'm glad to hear it. And her surgery went well?" Granny smiled.

"Yes, thanks for asking. You're so sweet to remember."

Her mother had a hip replacement a few weeks ago. I only knew because Granny had told me about it.

We put our purses and containers full of goodies on the table to be checked.

"Y'all brought goodies for today?" she asked, as she checked our IDs and then started checking our purses.

"We did." I uncovered everything so she could check. "Grab a few if you'd like."

"I will happily take one of each." She grabbed a napkin then helped herself to one of each type of cookie. "Thanks, y'all. You're all checked in."

She had us go through the metal detector and then we made our way back to the visitor room. We went to the table with our name on it, then waited. Granny Ines took the treats that we were sharing to the table and unpacked them. She started talking to another lady who was doing the same.

They looked like old friends as they laughed and hugged, then talked about each of the treats. I couldn't hear everything they said, but they were both animated so it must be good.

Auntie Rita pulled a tissue out of her purse, dabbing her eyes, then twisted it in her hand.

"You nervous?" I asked her.

"Yeah, but I have no reason to be. It isn't like I haven't done this same visit numerous times over the past ... what? Almost thirty years." She touched the tissue to her eyes again. "It just never gets easy to see your baby brother in a place like this."

"Yeah, I can understand. It hasn't been easy to see my loving father behind bars, either, well loving in the memory of a five-year-old."

"I'm sure. And he definitely loved you."

"I know." I smiled, taking her hand.

The buzzer rang signaling the prisoners would be coming. My stomach flip-flopped a bit as they started to come in. Partially because of the topic I wanted to bring up. Last time I had talked to my father about a case, he ended up in the infirmary.

"Tito! Mijo!" Granny waved as he came around the corner. He had to stay in line until he was fully in the room.

"My little Tito," Rita called to him. She had called him that my entire life, and I think possibly his entire life. He was her little Tito. She used to tell me how she would play dress up with him when he was a toddler, saying he was the best baby doll.

"Mamma! Rita. Hello!" He waved back. Then he saw me and his smile widened. "Jessie! Oh, you came today."

When he said my name, a man I didn't know looked right at me. His face was hard and his dark eyes stared right through me. A shiver went through my body.

As soon as they allowed it, he rushed to us, hugging us each in turn. I forgot all about the man as I got to hug my father for the first time in a few months.

When the greeting was over, he saw the tray of cookies and blondies. His eyes went wide.

"Mine?"

"Of course, mijo." Granny smiled. "All your favorites."

He snagged a polvorones in one hand and an oatmeal cookie in the other. His smile was so big.

"This is the best." He took a bite of one and then the other. "How are you, Jessie? It has been a bit since I've gotten a visit with you."

"Yeah, sorry about that. I should have more time after the holidays."

"Oh, why's that?"

"I promoted one of my line cooks so she can now step into the head chef position while I'm off or doing projects. I am thinking we might start having a booth at the art festivals."

This was the first time I was verbalizing my plans to have a booth, but I thought it was time to finally jump in.

"Oh, I miss going to those festivals."

"They've gotten much bigger than when we were kids or even teens," Rita said.

"I can imagine." He grabbed a crinkle cookie and then another oatmeal one. "What else is going on?"

I looked at Granny and Auntie Rita. At least I no longer had to worry about them overhearing my conversation. They were in support of me asking him questions.

I just had to worry about anyone else hearing me. I looked around. Everyone was engrossed in their own conversations.

"I was telling her how Mikey Stokes used to be in here," Granny whispered. "And, you heard about him being killed, executed basically."

"Yeah, I did hear. Are you looking into his murder?" Dad asked, his eyes darting around to see who was watching. The guards usually frowned on this type of gossip, but we didn't have one currently in earshot.

"I am," I whispered. Nobody seemed to give a sideways look, so I continued. "What can you tell me about Mikey?"

"That guy was a troublemaker with a capital T. Always getting in fights. Usually he started it by running his mouth then not knowing when to stop."

"Tell her about your run in with him," Granny said.

"Oh, yeah, he was popping off about me having a temper and no self-control."

"That's all it took for you to hit him?"

"No, I mean, yes, but he was like a dog with a bone. Just wouldn't let it go. Anytime he saw me, he'd call me ... well, a lot of racial slurs. One day, I just had enough and so I punched him. He might have been a small guy, but he was wily and nimble."

"He did a number on his stepdaughter a few weeks back," I said, my blood pressure raising just thinking about how awful she'd looked that night I picked her up and took her to the hospital.

"That Shayla girl?" Dad asked.

"Yeah, she has been put under my guardianship, at least until she turns eighteen, but she lives with Vee and I now."

"What happened to Sawyer?"

"He's engaged and living with his girlfriend Riley now, or I guess fiancée, not girlfriend. It is a fairly new thing." I smiled.

"She's a sweet girl, but a little blunt for my taste," Granny said.

"I agree. She is polite and thoughtful, but she doesn't have a filter," Auntie Rita added.

"Sounds like I would like her and sounds just like Sawyer's type." Dad laughed.

"Ha, yeah, I guess he has always liked strong, independent women." I smiled, thinking about my longtime friend. I then lowered my voice again, "What do you know about Ezra Lloyd?"

"Ezra? He thinks we're friends or something. I cannot stand that little twit." He gave me a thumbs down. "He is actually over there."

Dad nodded his head to a table across the room. I tried to look over without *looking*. It was the man from earlier. He was sitting with a woman. I wonder if that was Trina.

I'd have to remember to really keep my voice down.

"But what is he like? Anything between him and Mikey?"

"They were cellmates. That was back before Mikey was with Kenna and the twins were infants. Mikey got out and Ezra still had several years left on his sentence. Mikey saw an opportunity with her. Then when Ezra found out that not only did Mikey hook up with his girl, but that Mikey was around his baby girls, he went crazy. He swore he would get him back, some day."

"Wow. Do you think he could have hired someone?"

Officer Martindale was walking around, ensuring everyone was following the rules. He cleared his throat when he heard our conversation. It was a warning for us to be careful what we were discussing.

"Not likely. As I was going to say, they listen to our calls, it would be difficult." He looked over at Officer Martindale who grinned and winked our way. Dad offered him a little salute. "I get it, Martindale."

We talked about the cookies until the officer moved back across the room.

"Well, that's disappointing. I was hoping to solve this for Shayla. She's a suspect."

"What are your clues?"

"Not much. Just a note stuffed under their mattress and then a short list of names. Nothing to go on, but with Mikey stealing Ezra's family, I guess I could see that as motive."

There was a sound behind me. It was Officer Martindale clearing his throat. I had missed him coming back over.

This whole conversation probably sounded like we were plotting something, but it would only sound like that out of context. I seriously just wanted to know about who could have killed Kenna and Mikey.

Dad looked at him, shooting him some kind of look. Officer Martindale then crossed to the other side of the room, flashing some kind of hand gesture dad's way. That was impressive. I guess dad had some kind of clout around here after all these years.

It had me wondering if Ezra had any of that kind of power.

"Okay, look. I will ask around and I can get some special phone time once I have more information. See if we can't get this solved for you and what was her name again?"

"Shayla."

"Right, Shayla. Ezra thinks of her as his kid, too. He has pictures of them and talks about her as sweetly as he does his own girls."

"Really?"

He looked over to Ezra. "Yeah. I think that's why he thinks we are friends. Both girl dads. That's his girlfriend, by the way. His mother and the twins are supposed to visit him tomorrow."

I tried to glance without seeming obvious. Did he know Shayla was living with me? Probably. Maybe that's why he gave me such a once over look when they'd come in.

"He didn't seem happy to see me when y'all came in," I said.

"Really?" Dad looked over. Ezra did a head nod thing when he saw dad looking. "He seems okay. Maybe he was just curious about who Shayla is living with. Plus, you're my daughter. We're all curious about each other's family and lives outside of here."

"I guess."

Officer Martindale was starting to make his way back around the room to our side. It was time for a change of subject. I had all I needed anyway.

"Now on to different topics, some good news, actually. My lawyer called me the other day. They are looking at reducing my sentence."

"Really?"

"What? How?"

"Oh, mijo!" Granny clapped her hands together.

That would be amazing. Dad went on to explain about how with overcrowding and his good behavior, well, okayish behavior, they were considering him to have the reduced sentence.

"I could be out sometime in the next year or two."

If it happened, I would get my father back and a second chance with him. I didn't want to hope. It would just leave me disappointed if it didn't happen.

"Five minutes. Five more minutes." The announcement came over the speaker.

We wrapped up our visit with a little family news and gossip, then gave hugs. Dad was allowed to keep the cookies, so when they had the prisoners line up, we just watched him and then walked out. I felt suddenly empty and alone, even with my grandmother and aunt nearby.

Auntie Rita looped her arm through mine. She smiled at me with tears in her eyes. She didn't have to say it because I was feeling it too. The leaving was the hardest part.

Once in the car, we settled in for the long drive home. We all processed the visit, mostly in silence. I had a lot to think about, not only with Shayla's case, but my father's, now.

I can't hope. I can't have expectations, I thought.

Chapter Fifteen

After school, Shayla and her friends came bursting in, giggling and talking over each other. I had just gotten home myself. Thankfully, even though it was Friday, things at the restaurant weren't as crazy. Just normal crazy.

"Oh, hey Jess," Shayla said when she saw me.

"Hi. How was school?"

"Fine. I got an A on that test."

"I knew you would."

"You know Brooklynne, and this is Macy."

"Nice to meet you, Macy. Hi, Brooklynne."

"Hi, Chef," Brooklynne said.

"Jess. Please call me Jess." I smiled.

"Okay, Jess," Brooklynne said with a smile.

"How are things over at Beaks and Brews?"

"Different. Fast. Chef Nathan is a good mentor though."

I'd known Chef Nathan for several years. He was a good chef. Not as patient, but knowledgeable and ran a good business. I was glad to hear he had taken on some of the students.

"What about you, Macy? How is your school going?" I asked, trying to include her. She was the only non-culinary student.

She was enrolled in the cosmetology school at the high school and had given Shayla haircuts and washed her hair when she had needed it. If only everyone had a friend as caring back in high school.

It made me think of my own *"ride or die"* friend, Vee, who would be home any minute. She would give me the shirt off her back, if we were the same size. I would do the same for her.

"It's good, and I just got my first salon job. I start on Monday."

"Oh, that's exciting."

"Yeah, it isn't as interesting as working in a restaurant. I'll just be answering phones, sweeping up, and things like that, but it's a start."

"Yes, it sounds like a good start."

"Well, unless you need something, we're going up to my room." She squealed. "My room! It is so beautiful."

"Go. Have fun!"

They ran up the stairs laughing the entire way.

Oh, to be young again. I chuckled to myself.

A few hours later, Vee was home, and we were just hanging out in the kitchen. There were homemade pizzas in the oven. I had made a bunch of dough, then let the girls top their own. Once they were in the oven, we set a timer. I was cleaning up the mess left behind by the girls.

As I wiped up the counter, I turned to look at my friend. Vee was innocently sitting there scrolling through her phone. I leaned over thinking how much her friendship means to me and reminiscing with myself about us as teenagers.

"What?" Vee asked, shooting me an ugly look.

"Just thinking about how much I love you."

"I love you, too, you big weirdo." She blew me a kiss. She pointed up to where the girls were giggling and jumping around, probably doing one of those Tik Tok dances. "You thinking of her and her friends?"

"Yeah, I'm just glad she has people who stand by her, just like I have." I reached for my friend's hand.

"Me too, but don't forget you've been there for me, too."

"You have no problems. What have I done for you?"

"Um, hello, my hair! Dex got the nice hair, and I got this." She pulled at her wild locks.

It was true. Her brother had won in that gene pool. His hair was beautiful, but then again, he took really good care of it. He had all the products.

Vee is more of a wash and go girl, even though she didn't have wash and go hair. Her hair needs a decent conditioner and maybe a satin bonnet. I have bought her probably a dozen over the years, but she never uses them. Or maybe for a few days. Then they end up at the bottom of her sock drawer.

"Yeah, but if you would listen to me, it wouldn't require as much work daily."

The timer went off on the oven. There were squeals from upstairs, and three pairs of thundering feet came running down.

"Are the pizzas done?" Shayla asked, her face bright and relaxed in a way I hadn't seen yet. She looked her age for once, not like a person weighed down with too much responsibility and drama for her age.

"I don't know, chef, check." I teased her.

"Oh, duh!" She pulled open the oven, grabbing an oven mitt to pull them out. "Done! Dinner is served."

The girls cheered. Vee and I exchanged a look. Sometimes I felt young still, then I was around young people, and I felt all thirty-five, almost thirty-six years. Which, yes, is still young, but it isn't teenager young.

Shayla expertly cut the pizzas and plated it for her guests and us.

"This is awesome."

"Thanks, Shay!"

The pizzas had turned out good. Vee and I had a few pieces, but the girls ate every bite and were looking for more. We had a few bags of chips and popcorn, but I was out of pizza dough.

"Well, I made a strawberry crunch cheesecake," Shayla offered.

I had watched her do it. It was impressive. She was talented. I couldn't wait for the competition in a few weeks, so she could show off for a bigger audience.

"Wait? *The* cheesecake?" Brooklynne asked.

"That very one."

"What's this about 'the cheesecake'?" Macy asked.

"I made it in class, and everyone gobbled it up." Shayla said proudly. "Mr. Jones had me make him one to take home for Ms. Beverly."

"Oh, then I can't wait to have some. Where is it?" Macy looked around.

Shayla went to the fridge and pulled it out.

"Ta-da!"

We clapped and cheered, as Shayla started cutting and serving each of us a slice.

"This is amazing!" Brooklynne said. "I can't bake like this at all."

"So good."

Once the cheesecake was eaten, I told the girls I would clean up so they could get started on their next fun activity.

They ran back up to Shayla's room. The music started up and the thumps and bumps on the ceiling began again.

"Do you want help?" Vee asked me.

"Just keep me company."

"Can do." She took a seat at the island. "I'm so glad that Shayla is getting this experience. Everyone deserves to have fun experiences."

"I have been thinking the same. It is so fun to watch her be a kid and laugh, be relaxed."

"This case is weird." She looked over her shoulder at the office.

We still only had a few things on the murder board this time. In the past, we had several more clues, or names at least. This time it was nearly blank, and even the ones we had seemed to be dead ends.

My dad had called earlier but hadn't gotten any information for me yet. He said he was still going to try. I knew he just wanted to help, but being in prison didn't truly give him much freedom to do so.

"Yeah, we have almost nothing still. I mean, the others had been challenging, but somehow, I got it. This one … nothing."

I put the last dish in the dishwasher, added a pod, then ran it. I looked around.

"Done. Movie?" I asked.

"Yep."

We grabbed some wine and headed to the living room. As soon as we plopped down, both of our phones sent a notification.

"Is that the front door camera?" I asked, pulling out my phone.

"Yeah, sounded like it."

There was a dark shadow of a person creeping by Shayla's car. They stuck something on the window. I got up, running to the front door to turn on the porch light, watching the camera the entire time. The person jumped and ran off.

Their face was covered, and they were wearing an oversized jacket. Probably in an effort to make themselves seem larger.

"Well, that's scary," Vee said coming to stand by me.

"I better call this in." I stared at my phone. "Do I call 9-1-1, Raff, or Detective Upton?"

"Just try Rafferty."

I hit his number. It rang only twice before he answered.

"Hey, Jess. What's up?"

"We just caught someone sneaking around outside and they left something on Shayla's car."

"What is it?"

"I don't know. I didn't want to go outside just yet. What if they are still there or what if the item is harmful?"

"Good point. Okay, I'm on my way and I'll call for backup. Hang tight."

We hung up and looked over at Vee.

"I should tell Shayla." I headed upstairs, hesitating before knocking on the door. What was I going to say? Well, obviously the truth, but I didn't want to scare her. I knocked.

"Come in," Shayla said.

I pushed the door open. She was painting Macy's nails and Brooklynne was watching, while blowing on her own nails.

I plastered a smile on my face, so as not to alarm her. "Um, I don't know how to say this, so I'll just say it. Someone was just poking around outside and they put something on your car."

She froze, staring at me.

"What? What did they put on my car?"

"I don't know. The police are on the way."

"Are they still out there? Are we in danger?" Brooklynne asked, her eyes wide.

"They ran off, but the police should be here any second."

"You're sure we are safe?"

"Of course." But I was starting to wonder if I should get a dog. I loved Lulu but she didn't bark when there was danger.

"We should go wait downstairs."

The girls comforted each other as we waited, but thankfully, it wasn't long before the front door camera sent us a notification followed by a knock at the door.

"Hey, Raff," I said opening it. He was accompanied by Officer Roberts and Officer Wright. Roberts and Wright were in their uniform, while Rafferty wasn't.

"Hey, okay, so we have secured the scene, and this is what was left on the car."

It was a handwritten note.

I warned them and you see what happened.
Now stop looking.

Vee read it along with me, then I passed it to Shayla. She gasped.

"This looks like the same handwriting."

"Same handwriting as what?" Raff asked.

"A note we found cleaning out their house." Then I really wished I hadn't said any of this out loud. The cat was out of the bag now. "Do you want to see it?"

"We are going to try to get prints," Roberts said. He and Wright walked back to the car.

"I'll look at it," Rafferty said, then stepped inside.

Vee, Shayla and I exchanged a look. Were we really going to show him our secret? Yes, Detective Upton knew about it and helped us organize it better, at least on a past case. Did we really want more of the officers to know about it?

Too late now.

"Okay, before I show you this, I need to tell you that Detective Upton does know I do this."

"What? Your murder board? Yeah, we all know about it. I have been dying to see it." He gestured. "This way?"

"Oh, um, yeah."

We all walked to the office. It was so empty now without all of Shayla's stuff in it, but the board was all we needed anyway.

"Wow, nice. I have always wanted to make one of these."

"Upton said these aren't really used except for maybe a little brainstorming."

"Yeah, pretty much."

He studied each paper, taking down the other handwritten note.

"Where did you say you found this?"

"We were helping clean out Kenna and Mikey's house. After it was cleared by the police of course."

He nodded, then studied the two papers.

"Yeah, this does look the same. It looks to be feminine handwriting."

"How can you tell?" Vee leaned over to look at it closer.

"Well, it isn't completely perfect technique to tell, but look how the letters are round, even, and evenly spaced. A man's or masculine handwriting tends to be hurried, uneven, and spiked."

"Interesting."

"Can I see the security footage?"

"Yeah, they hid their body well, so it is hard to see who it is or any specific body features," I said, as I pulled up the app on my phone. I rewound to just before the person came into frame. "Here."

He watched, then watched it twice more.

"Yeah, they really hid their body and face well. No distinguishing characteristics."

"So now what?" I asked.

"Now I go check in with the other two to see what they think. I'll also ask Chief if we can add an extra patrol or two past your house."

"That will be helpful. Thank you."

He handed me my phone back and the two notes. "I'll be right back."

I stuck the notes on the board, then looked at them.

"Well, that sure put a damper on my first sleepover," Shayla said. Her two friends hugged her.

"It's okay."

"I'm still having fun."

"Yeah?"

"Of course. Plus, this is really cool." Macy pointed at the board. "Is this how you have figured out the other murders?"

"I guess you heard about those." I flinched.

"Everybody has heard about it. It's amazing!" Brooklynne said.

"Thanks," I said unsure if that was the right response. "Well, I think y'all can get back to nails and whatever else you were doing."

"You sure?" Shayla asked.

"Yeah, if we need you again, I'll let you know. Go. Have fun."

The girls left. No giggling this time but I could hear them turn on music again once they were upstairs.

"What do you think?" Vee asked.

"I honestly don't know." I turned to look at the board again. There weren't any female suspects, so I guess that ruled out everyone on our list.

"Kyle did say his handwriting analysis was not fool proof, so it could be a man who wrote it, or someone could have asked someone else to write it."

"Yeah, that's what I'm starting to think now. Maybe Ezra's current girlfriend?"

"Maybe, but I wonder why she would? No real motive for either of them, is there?"

"Except for Mikey basically stealing Ezra's family."

"Yeah, I think I'd be hella mad about someone stealing my family like that," Vee said.

"Hella? Really?"

"I tried a thing." She shrugged.

We walked back to the kitchen and took a seat at the island until the officers were done outside.

"Knock, knock," Kyle said coming back in. He saw me and his face brightened. "Roberts and Wright are taking the prints back to the station. We need the note though."

"Do I have time to make a copy of it?"

He looked over his shoulder. "Yeah, hurry."

I ran to the office, threw it on the printer, copier, fax combo, and hit the copy button. It spit out a perfect replica of the note. I grabbed the original from the glass and took it to Rafferty.

"Here you are."

"Thanks." Our hands touched as he took it from me. He smiled. "After I give them this, want me to stay for a bit? Just in case."

I looked over at Vee. She smiled and nodded.

"Yeah, that would be nice."

"Great. I'll be right back."

He stayed for about an hour. It made me feel better having him here. When he left, I made sure the alarm was set, and the girls were safe in

Shayla's room. But the idea of a woman suspect had me tossing and turning all night.

Chapter Sixteen

It was nearly noon on Thanksgiving Day. The restaurant was crowded with customers and the employees were hustling, but the vibe was jovial and festive.

Customers seemed to like the menu that we'd planned. People got to choose either turkey, ham or combo, plus sides. Every table got a basket of rolls and a small crock of cranberry sauce. For dessert, there was a choice between pumpkin or pecan pie.

"This was a great idea, Chef," Hannah said. "My parents had the best time. Mom said it was the best Thanksgiving."

Hannah had just come back to the kitchen from visiting with them for a few minutes. My family should be here any minute so I would get my turn to visit shortly.

"I'm so glad to hear it." I plated another round of turkey, passing it to her so she could add the sides to it.

"Chef, this is amazing!" Marco said as he came to grab plates from me. "Selene and mamma just left. They wanted me to thank you for doing this."

That became the theme from my entire staff. I had worked the past two days roasting turkeys and smoking the hams. Parker had helped me while Hannah organized the line cooks and prep cooks into making all the sides. June had worked on appetizers and rolls.

Of course, the desserts were all made by Natalie and Shayla. Ripley and Maxine, my two bartenders, had worked on some special drinks.

"Mocktails are the new black." Ripley laughed when he presented their three new drink ideas. They had a cranberry iced tea, a raspberry lime soda, and cranberry orange mocktail.

"Any of these can have alcohol added to them, too," Maxine added.

"Nice. I love them."

It had been a fun week as we all came together to make this happen. Everyone had been so excited and the energy around the restaurant was cheerful.

"Hey, Chef, your aunt and grandmother are here," Ava yelled to me. "They're the sweetest."

"Thanks. Tell them I'll be just a minute."

I finished the plates I was currently working on, then turned the station over to Hannah. I washed my hands, smoothed my hair, then went to the dining room to find my auntie and granny.

When I walked out to the dining room, there was Christmas music playing through the speakers. People all around were chatting, laughing, and eating. Every table was full of smiling families and friends.

Customers saw me and started yelling hellos and praise.

"Chef! Hey, Chef Jessica."

"Oh, there she is. Hi, Chef!"

"Thank you for hosting this. Everything is excellent."

"I had been dreading the holiday, but this has been so much fun."

I smiled and thanked them for coming and wished them all a Happy Thanksgiving.

Finally, I made it to my family's table. They were enjoying some pimento cheese dip and toast.

"Oh, Jessie!" Auntie Rita turned, smiling at me.

"Mija, hello, this is amazing," Granny Ines said, patting the seat next to her.

I took a seat. "What did you order?"

"I got turkey with dressing, green beans and corn," Auntie Rita said.

"I got the ham with mashed potatoes and the roasted Brussel sprouts. We thought we could split."

"You can get a combination, but yeah, you can split."

"Yes, we talked about that, but anyway, here we are." Granny shrugged.

"This mocktail is delicious," Auntie Rita said. "I have always loved cranberry and orange together, and just a touch of lime."

We visited a few more minutes until their entrées arrived, so I said goodbye.

Since I'd run through when I first came out, I decided to walk around to each table to greet the families and friends of my staff. After a few tables, I came to one with very familiar faces.

"Detective Upton, Brooke. So nice to see you. Hi, Aiden."

His little face lit up and he jumped up in the booth, holding his little hands up to me. "Chef Jess!"

I was so surprised by his reaction, but I picked him up, hugging him.

"Are you having fun?"

"Yes. Yes."

"Do you want to go see in the kitchen?" I hadn't had a chance yet to do this with him, and in hindsight, I should have asked his parents first.

"Yes!" he yelled, pointing over my shoulder.

"Sorry, I should have asked."

"It's fine. He will love it," Brooke said.

"He loves to play kitchen, so it will be fun for him to see a real commercial kitchen," Rich smiled, as he fed little Evie.

At nearly six months old, she was still too young to understand about being a chef or playing kitchen.

"Great. We'll be right back."

With that, I carried my little friend into the kitchen for a quick tour. He giggled a little louder the closer we got to the kitchen area.

Once in the kitchen, he asked so many questions and pointed to everything shiny.

"Mixer! Oh, fridge. We see the fridge?"

"Yes, of course." I took him into the large walk-in refrigerator.

"Brr, cold."

"Yes, it's cold in here."

"Look, lettuce. 'Matoes!"

"Yes, we use those for salad, burgers, and sandwiches."

"Yummy."

"Who is this little cutie?" Natalie asked when we came out of the fridge.

"This is Aiden Upton, future chef."

"Oh, is he that cute detective's son?"

"Ha, yes, and his wife and this one's mother is waiting for me to bring him back."

"I can still think he is cute, even if he is married." She laughed as I walked away.

I handed Aiden back to his parents, and stopped by a few more tables before my eyes focused on a specific table. There was Lynn with Ivy and Dove.

I didn't know they were coming.

When I walked to their table, they were coloring together. Lynn was smart to bring a pad of paper and some crayons with her.

"Hi, Ms. Lynn. Ivy, Dove. Did you eat yet or just get here?"

"We just got here," Lynn said through tight lips. "The girls really wanted to come, and it doesn't make sense for me to make a big lunch with it just being the three of us."

"Oh, what happened to … um, Trina?" Trina was Ezra's girlfriend and last I heard she was living with Lynn and the girls to help out.

"She's history."

"Yeah, she and grandma got in a fight, then packed her stuff and left," Ivy said. Dove giggled next to her.

Lynn gave them a stern look.

"Well, I'm sorry to hear that. I'll go tell Shayla y'all are here. I know she'll want to see the girls."

"Hmph," Lynn said, smoothing her navy-colored blouse.

I straightened my back, leaning forward and lowering my voice. "Look, I get it, you're bitter about having to uproot your life, but can you for one second imagine what all of this might be like for Shayla or even these two girls? They miss their sister and their mother. Even if you don't like how Kenna was living her life, she was still their mother and -" I stopped myself from saying murdered. I didn't know how much the girls knew.

"Murdered," Ivy said, flatly. "Mama and Daddy Mikey were murdered."

Dove nodded.

"Well, okay. That." I stood up fully. "Just be respectful of them for that."

She sat there staring at me, then composed herself. "Fine, but can you think how I feel? My son is in prison for at least fifteen more years. These girls will be grown by then. And that man… the things he was doing, the things these innocent girls heard. I am glad they are now away from him."

Before we could speak more, Ivy yelled. "Shayla!!! There she is. Shay, over here."

We all turned. Dove started bouncing up and down in her chair. Shayla turned with a smile, then came over wrapping her arms around both girls at once.

"Hey, girlies! I missed you both so much. Gosh, you've gotten big. I thought I said no growing up too fast." The sisters laughed. "Hi, Grandma Lynn."

"Hi, Shayla," she said reluctantly, arms crossed over her chest. "It's nice to see you."

"May I sit for a minute?" She looked at both me and Lynn.

We both nodded.

"I'm going to head back to the kitchen." I looked at the family. "Y'all have a Happy Thanksgiving."

I walked away, stopping at a few tables to greet guests, but keeping an eye on Shayla and Lynn. The tension was heavy, but I could see it melting a bit with the excitement from the younger sisters. Even Lynn was smiling some by the time I made it to the kitchen door.

When I got back in the kitchen, everyone was talking about our little guest.

"Aiden sure is a cutie."

"When can we hire him?"

"Future chef indeed."

"I couldn't believe he knew some of the equipment names," Eli said. I laughed as I got back to my station.

Shayla came back with a huge smile on her face. That made me happy to see. I had been worried about her.

The next few hours flew by with the holiday cheer in the air. Now it was nearly the end of my shift, and our evening employees would be coming in soon.

I was happy to see we still had plenty of food, which was the best part of taking reservations - we could plan how much to cook. We had even cooked extra turkey because the plan for Friday's special was a turkey pot pie with an arugula salad on the side.

"Hey, Chef. Some more police officers are here. They asked for you," Skye said.

"Oh, okay, thanks." I looked over at Eli. Hannah was on a break. He nodded, so I knew he had my station. I turned to reply. "I'll be right there."

I washed my hands, checked my hair, then headed out to greet the officers. I hoped Kyle Rafferty was in this group. I mean that had to be why they were asking for me.

I guess it could be Officer Lupe Perez. She and I were friends too, but I'd already seen Detective Upton and he would be the only other person that might ask for me.

Stepping into the dining room, it was just as crowded as it had been all day. The music was still playing, and I noticed that a few tables had been pushed together.

Whatever it took for them to enjoy their holiday and meal.

"Jess, hey, Jess," I heard Rafferty call out.

My smile filled my whole face as I walked to his table. He was seated with Roberts, Perez, and the new officer, Wright. Kyle stood when I got to them. He leaned over to hug me.

"Hey."

"This is great." He gestured around. "Perfect idea, especially for those of us that have to work."

"Thanks."

Perez and Roberts both stood, giving me a hug, too.

"Thanks for doing this today, Jess," Lupe said.

"It really does mean a lot to us to have a place to go when we still have to work," Officer Tommy Roberts said.

All the officers' meals were on the house. I'd also offered it to any postal workers, even though neither Vee nor Sawyer would be able to make it today. They were going to their respective parents' houses.

"I'm glad I could do this." I smiled, then took a seat to visit with them for a few minutes while they waited for their food.

When it arrived, I stood.

"I'll let you get to your food."

I started to walk away, but Rafferty stopped me.

"Hey, what time do you get off today?" he whispered to me.

"Around three."

"Okay, my shift ends around six. I'll call you after."

"Sounds good."

He squeezed my hand before letting me walk away. I smiled all the way back to the kitchen. It was nearly three and the next shift started to show up.

"Hey, Chef, how was the day?" Parker asked as he came over drying his hands.

"Perfect. Wonderful. Everything ran like clockwork."

"Great. I'm excited for this. My parents will be coming shortly."

We traded places with him taking over the station. I went to clean my hands, then did one last round through the dining room.

Then before I left, I checked in with Shayla. She and Natalie would both be working until close but thankfully we were closing early tonight, with the last reservation being at six. The plan was to be closed around seven.

Once home, I fell back on our couch with my feet up. It was a great day. Low stress and the perfect way to celebrate the holiday. Still, it was a lot of work, I was glad it was behind me.

I guess I fell asleep because I woke up when Vee came bursting in.

"Honey, I'm home!" With Sawyer gone, I didn't hear that as often. "Oh, I'm sorry, were you sleeping?"

"I must have been." I rubbed my eyes. "How were things at the Paz house this year?"

"Wonderful. Mom made all my favorites. Oh, and Dex brought a girl home."

"Oh, my! Do we know her?"

"No, someone he met in Pinehurst."

"Did you like her?"

"Still too early to tell, but she seemed okay." She headed to the kitchen. "Mom sent leftovers! Lots of leftovers."

I watched as she unpacked containers and tubs into our fridge.

"She really sent a lot."

"She knows I live with two chefs but still thinks I'm going to starve. Look at me, I'm overweight as it is."

"No, you're not," I insisted.

"You're so kind, but yes, why else am I the only one without someone?"

"Um, you get plenty of attention? What happened with Elias? Haven't y'all been texting?" I said as I started us some hot water for tea.

Elias had helped out with Shayla's tires a couple of weeks ago, and they had reconnected. I know she has been texting with him since.

"Yes, but he hasn't asked me out." She pouted.

The front door opened and in came Shayla. She was all smiles.

"Oh, hey, y'all. Waiting for me?" She laughed. "Natalie let me leave early."

"That was nice of her! Want some tea?" I asked.

"That would be nice." She handed me a few papers. "Look at the drawings the girls gave me."

"These are good." I read Ivy on one and Dove on the other. The date had been added to each. But then my eyes went wide when I saw the handwriting on them.

"Who wrote their names here?" I pointed to the neat, round handwriting.

"Um, it looks like Grandma Lynn wrote that." Then her head snapped to look at me. "Ohmygosh! Do you think…?"

"I do."

We both ran to the office. Vee followed us.

"What am I missing?"

Shayla pulled the threatening notes from the board. We held the drawings next to them.

"It's her," we said together.

Vee came over to look.

"Lynn Lloyd? Why would she risk losing the girls?"

"I don't think she did the killing, but I think she helped," I said. "I need to call Raff or Upton."

I ran to the living room to grab my phone. I scrolled to Kyle's name. He would be getting off any second.

"Hey, Jess. Is something wrong?"

"Kind of. You're still at work?"

"I am."

"Do you still have connections over at Milton County?"

"Um, yeah, why? What's up?"

I explained about the drawings and what we suspected.

"I wondered if you can ask someone to check the phone conversations between Ezra and Lynn right before Kenna and Mikey's murder?"

"Yes, but it won't be instant, especially on Thanksgiving."

"How long do you think it will take?"

"Maybe two or three days?"

I exhaled. "We can wait. They think they've gotten away with it, at least for now."

"Okay, let me make some calls and I'll call you later."

We hung up. I relayed to Shayla and Vee what he had said.

"And now we keep this secret until we know for sure."

"What is going to happen to Ivy and Dove?" Shayla said.

None of us knew, but at least we now had an idea of who had killed Kenna and Mikey. It wasn't a drug deal gone wrong or Bobo, Hawk or some other no name person. It was likely Ezra, Lynn, and the person they hired.

Chapter Seventeen

It was two days before Rafferty called to let me know about the conversations. He actually asked to come talk in person. I agreed then called Hannah to let her know I wouldn't be in this morning.

H: **I have you covered, Chef!**

Me: **Thanks. Team Work.**

Now, Vee and I were pacing the floor, literally, as my nerves took over and my mind ran through every crazy scenario. Not sure why this case felt so much more important, because it wasn't any more or less so than ones in the past.

I think it was simply because I had to wait for them to investigate my hunch. The past few, the killer revealed themselves. Now, it felt like the killer or killers felt they were getting away with all of it, so why should they make a move now?

Thankfully, Shayla had slept over at Macy's last night and was still there this morning. I saw no reason for her to stay home while we waited. She would be just as safe at Macy's as she was here.

"This is bad, right? It feels bad," I said. Just the simple fact he wanted to give me the answer here felt weird or wrong.

"I'm sure it's fine, and we'll have an answer soon."

"But what if I'm wrong? What if the killer is never found and they keep threatening Shayla?"

"But what if you are right? What if you save her life?"

We got back to pacing, no more words spoken for several minutes.

There was a knock at the door breaking the silence. Vee and I whipped around to face each other.

"Well, this is it," I said with hope. I swung the door open to find Officers Rafferty and Roberts, Detective Upton, plus Chief Stone and Harlow and Darren Wilcox. "Um, hello?"

Chief Stone walked right in without a word, causing Vee to jump back. He marched into the kitchen, walking in a circle before turning to face us.

I looked back and forth between him and the group standing outside. After a pregnant pause, I snapped back to reality and gestured for the others to come in.

"Can I get anyone a drink?" I asked.

They all declined.

"We'll get to the point," Chief said. "You were right."

"I was right? About it being Lynn and Ezra?"

"Yes. They schemed to have them killed. It's all in the prison's transcripts," Chief grumbled.

He always seemed like he was in a bad mood. I suppose working on a Saturday morning would make one extra grumpy, especially when that person rarely worked on Saturday morning.

"I brought a printout of the transcript for you," Raff said, his tone professional as he handed it to me.

"Thanks." I started to flip through it, but Chief Stone started talking again. What I had read looked boring.

"You can read it later, but the short of it is, they spoke in code. On the day of the murder, someone named Froggy called and told Ezra the dog had been put to sleep."

"The dog? What dog?"

"It means that he had completed the job he was hired for."

"Oh." I should have realized that, but I was trying to read while he was talking. I gave up in favor of just listening. "What's next then? They get arrested?"

"Yes, but there is also the business of the girls," Detective Upton said. He looked over at Harlow and Darren.

"Obviously, I would take them, they are my nieces," Harlow said. I heard a but coming. "But our life is really busy, and it just wouldn't work out well for us." She looked at Darren, who looked down at his shoes.

No surprise, she wouldn't take any of her sister's children.

"So, what does that mean?" I knew what they meant, but I wanted to know what it meant for the girls.

Everyone got really quiet and awkward.

"They want Shayla to take custody of them, or well, you until she is officially eighteen," Rafferty finally said.

I looked at Vee. She nodded, a slow smile spreading across her face. This was not the outcome I was thinking.

"Absolutely. I would be happy to have them." Who was I turning into?

"Can we talk to Shayla about it, too? We want to ensure she knows what is happening," Detective Upton said.

"I know she will be thrilled and be an amazing guardian to them, but she isn't here. She spent the night at a friend's house."

"Which friend?" Harlow asked. "Will she be home soon?"

"A friend from school. I'll call her."

I hit her number.

"Hello." Her sleepy voice came through the phone.

"Hey, Shayla. Sorry, did I wake you?"

"Yeah, it's okay. What's up?" she asked.

"When do you think you'll head home?"

"I don't know. Macy is still asleep." There was a mumbling behind her. "Well, she's sort of asleep. Is something going on?"

I looked around the room. All the faces were staring at me.

"Half of the police department is here," I said. Rafferty was the only one who laughed at that. I knew it wasn't really half of the department, but the force was small, so it was still a significant number of them here. "Plus, your Aunt Harlow and Uncle Darren. They have confirmed Lynn and Ezra killed your mom."

"Oh, wow, really? Okay, I'll be home in less than ten."

"Okay, just be safe."

"I will. Oh, wait, what about Ivy and Dove?"

"That's part of what we are talking about now."

"Do we get them? Do I get custody?" She sounded excited. I knew she would want them.

"Yes, that's the plan at current."

"Woohoo! Okay, I'm on my way." She hung up.

I fought the urge to laugh, celebrate, get excited like she was.

"Um, she's on her way. Should be just about ten minutes, maybe."

Chief Stone crossed his arms over his chest, exhaling heavily. *Geez, dramatic much*, I thought.

"Great," Upton said.

"We can wait, I guess," Harlow said.

"Do y'all want to have a seat?" I pointed towards our kitchen table. It had seats for up to eight. "Can I get anyone a drink, now? I have Malory's coffee from Roasted Beans."

"Oh, yes, coffee please."

"Me too."

"Malory's? Yes, please."

"Great. I'll start the pot," I said. "Vee, help?"

We went into the kitchen to get everything together for our guests. I started the pot to brew while she got out mugs. We then worked together to carry all the mugs to the table.

We made small talk while we waited for Shayla. Ten minutes turned into fifteen which turned into twenty, and I started to walk the floor. Vee stood guard at our front window to watch for her car.

"Something isn't right," I mumbled.

"She probably just got held up at Macy's. You know how girls are," Vee said.

"We need to get going soon. We have kids that need to get to activities, and I have a book club this afternoon," Harlow said.

"Yeah, my wife will be wondering what happened to me," Chief Stone said.

"I'll call her," Vee volunteered. She hit the button on her phone. She listened to it but then said "voicemail. That's weird."

I went outside to look up and down the street. Rafferty, Upton, and Roberts followed.

"Do you think we should go search for her?" Roberts asked.

"I do, but Jess, what do you think?" Raff asked me.

I hated to stall for time if she was in trouble, but who would want to hurt her?

"Oh, bleep! Yes, let's go look."

"No, you stay here in case she shows up. We'll start working our way around town."

"Do you know where her friend Macy lives?"

"I can get the address."

I called Mr. Jones who got in touch with Ms. Kemper who was in charge of the cosmetology school. It took roughly ten minutes, but I had Macy's address which I then messaged to the officers. They had already left to see what they could find.

Harlow and Darren had also left, but not to look for Shayla.

"We really have to get on with our Saturday. Call me once you find her." Harlow waved as they drove away.

"I wouldn't give her those kids, even if she was the last relative," Chief Stone said, some of his gruff attitude melted. "I am going to head to the station so I can mobilize more officers and see if we can find her."

"Thanks," I mumbled.

A few minutes later, Rafferty called.

"Hey, so we got to Macy's house. Shayla's car is still here, but according to Macy and her parents, she left. Have you heard from her at all?"

"No, nothing." My heart tightened. "Did you check their camera?"

"We are gathering the footage now to see what happened. It doesn't show much on their cameras. It shows Shayla walking out, then it looks like someone calls her or something catches her eye. She walks off camera and that's it."

"That's it? She's just gone." I choked.

"No, no. I just meant, she was never visible again on their camera."

"So, now what?"

"Roberts is asking neighbors and I'm going to start asking them as well, but I wanted to give you an update."

"Let me know when you find her." I sobbed.

"I'm sorry, Jess, I will find her."

We hung up and I sobbed quietly into my hands. I felt so hopeless and so helpless. I should be out there looking for her, but they told me to stay. Honestly, it was smart for me to stay in case she did make it here somehow.

Another thirty minutes after that, my stomach was in knots. I was standing on our second step, just waiting and watching. This was not right. Something was really, really wrong. Vee came up next to me, handing me a bottle of water.

"She'll be okay," she said.

"I hope so, because …" That was all I could say. Tears started to fall down my face again.

A car came to a stop in front of our townhouse. Out jumped Mr. Duncan Jones and Mrs. Beverly Jones.

"Have you heard anything?" Bev asked.

"Nothing."

"How long since you last talked to her?" Duncan asked.

"About an hour." I looked over at Vee. She nodded.

"We're here for you," Bev said, coming to stand beside me on our tiny step, wrapping an arm around my waist.

We all stood there together for another a few minutes, just watching the street. The stray cat walked from under the bushes to stare at us from across the street. I had recently nicknamed him Baxter, but I couldn't find any humor in our staring contest today.

"I have an idea." I pulled out my phone, then scrolled to the contact I wanted.

"Hello, Jess," Cullen said when he answered.

"Cullen, I hope I didn't wake you."

"Not at all. What's going on?"

"I need your help." I explained what I needed him to do. "How long do you think it will take?"

"Give me about five to ten minutes to hack in, then another five or so minutes to find the right location and then I can track try to track any cars from there to see if one might tie back to her somehow."

We agreed that he would call me back when he found something.

"Do you think he can do it?" Vee asked.

"I do. I really do."

Especially since the police hadn't come up with anything yet and they have had plenty of time, at least in my opinion. Though my thoughts might be skewed at the moment since I was so worried about poor Shayla.

After a few minutes, we went inside to wait. Vee made more coffee, serving the Joneses. The three of them talked around me while I stared at my phone willing it to ring with good news.

Ring. Ring. RING!

Then it did ring. It was Cullen. The other three watched me hopefully as I answered.

"Hello, did you find anything?"

"Yes. I did." He started to describe how she walks out of the house and a man calls to her from two houses down. She walks his way, and he grabs her. "I followed his truck through town until it goes into the camo zone."

"Oh, bleep! I know where he took her. I know exactly where he took her. Thanks, Cullen. I'll call you back once I have her."

I hung up and looked at the eager faces in front of me.

"Let's go. I'll call the police on the way."

We jumped into my car, and I hit Rafferty's number as I drove down the road.

"Hey, Jess. Sorry, I —" He started to say.

"I know where she is. We're heading there now."

"You do? Where, so I can meet you?"

"Her old house."

"We'll be right there. Don't engage if you get there first."

I hung up and focused on driving.

"I hope we get there in time," Mr. Jones said.

"Even though the officer told us to stay out of it, I have every intention of going in," Bev said. "You know Duncan and I never had kids. I have always thought all the students are like our kids in a way. Troubled kids, sorry home lives, or just not catching any breaks in life. However they ended up in his class, we have tried to make them part of our family. Our Dashwood Culinary Arts Program family."

Tears formed in my eyes. "I always felt like you were like a mom and dad to us, too."

We pulled up to Shayla's old house to find that the police were taking two men out in handcuffs and Officer Perez was walking out with a crying Shayla.

I was surprised that the house was still standing, since Todd's company had bought all of these houses. Though I could see the notices on each of the doors. That meant demolition would start soon.

It meant nothing to me now. I was just glad to see Shayla walking out of the house and she didn't appear to be injured in any way.

I rushed out of the car. Everything and everyone around me blurred as I focused on getting to her.

"Shayla, oh my gosh, Shayla!"

"Jess!" We ran to each other, hugging tightly. Vee and the Joneses came up seconds later to join us.

"I'm so glad you are okay. You are okay, right?" I looked at her up and down, and side to side. It reminded me of my grandmother doing a body check when I had fallen down a set of stairs when I was seven. "You look okay."

"Yeah, I'm fine. They were waiting for the signal or something, but then they were supposed to kill me. The signal never came then the officers burst in."

"Who were they?"

"That's Froggy and Billy. Friends of Ezra's."

"They are the ones who killed your mom and Mikey?" It was part statement, part question.

"Yeah. We talked about it. They told me in too much detail what happened." Shayla started sobbing harder. I couldn't understand everything she was saying, but something about her mother begging for her life. "They said, she said, 'I can't leave my girls.' So, some of her last words were about me, Ivy, and Dove."

"Oh, Shayla, I'm sorry."

"No, you don't understand. It means she *did* love me. My mom loved me."

"Of course she did. Of course."

Rafferty came over to check on her. "You okay? Do you need medical attention?"

"No, I'm fine. They didn't hurt me."

"Okay, we'll need to do an interview with you, but I understand if you'd like to head home to rest now. We can interview you there."

"What about Ivy and Dove? I assume y'all will be arresting Lynn, too. That was what all of this was about wasn't it?" Shayla started to panic breathe. I stroked her hair to try and calm her.

"We have someone picking them all up now. We will bring the girls to you at Jess's, okay?"

"Okay, perfect. Thank you."

"Well, let's go home and wait for your sisters."

"I can fix up your old room for them!" Vee said.

With that the three of us went home to get ready for our new cute little roommates. The future was never going to be the same.

Chapter Eighteen

"Ivy, stop looking at me," Dove yelled over me.

"I'm away over here," Ivy countered, also across me.

"Shh, now, Shayla's group will be coming out any minute. You want to support your sister, right?"

"Yeah," they agreed.

It had been nearly two weeks since we got custody of Ivy and Dove. Technically, Shayla, now eighteen years and two days old, was the guardian but she asked me for help.

"I'm not ready to be on my own with them. Heck, I am hoping you'll still be my new mom."

"Um, not sure about the mom part but I'm definitely up for the big sister role."

"Who acts like a mom." She giggled.

We fixed up the office for the girls. Vee had a special power and got two twin beds, a new dresser, and a closet full of clothes, all before the police and child protection services brought us the girls after Lynn had been taken into custody.

We'd also gotten the murder board cleared. Shayla added some posters that her friends, Brooklynne and Macy brought over for the little girls. Shayla had added all of their old things she had packed from their old house and her friends had also brought some new stuffed animals and toys for them.

By the time the girls arrived, it looked like it had always been their room.

I knew their world had been turned upside down. I remember my own father's arrest and how much had changed in my life. They not only lost their home and mother, but now their grandmother. It was a lot for anyone, but especially children who couldn't understand grown-up problems.

They had cried almost non-stop the first day and night. Shayla had done her best to comfort them, but after her near-death experience, she was emotionally spent herself. The three sisters sat in the little girls' room and cried together, then fell asleep only to start it again the next day. By dinnertime on day two, everyone was a lot calmer.

I made homemade chicken fingers, macaroni and cheese with a side of green beans. These weren't canned green beans warmed on the stove. No, they were not. I roasted them with a drizzle of olive oil along with some onion and garlic, then seasoned them with salt and pepper, then topped it all with crispy bacon.

I didn't know if they were picky eaters or not, but I tried a thing, and it seemed to work. Vee and I watched in awe as the two skinny little girls gobbled down every bite and asked for more, especially the green beans.

"These are the best green beans ever," Ivy had declared. Dove kept shoving them in her mouth and could only nod in agreement.

Shayla smiled for the first time in days.

Now, we were in Florida for the week for the 41st Annual Culinary Arts High School Competition for the Old Hollywood Glam themed competition. Shayla had already made it through the first three rounds. Now she was in the finals. In just a few hours, we would know if she won. It would be a huge win too.

This year was a cash prize of $10,000 in each of the categories. There were three, appetizer, entree, and dessert. Shayla was, of course, competing in the dessert round.

She hadn't yet decided on college or more specifically a culinary school, but for now, the plan was for her to continue to work and save. Plus, she had her sisters to think of now. Raising them would take a lot of her time, but she had a village to help her.

Granny Ines passed each girl a piece of hard candy, then winked at me. She had told me it was the secret to keep little kids quiet. I don't know if I believed it, but they did settle down.

Granny, Auntie Rita, Vee, Sawyer, and Riley had all come along for the trip. We had rented a large house not far from Disney World, and the plan before we headed home was to hit each park. Vee had even bought the little girls princess dresses to wear.

This is why she'd quickly become their favorite person. I had to play disciplinarian and Shayla was big sister.

They'd also both taken a huge liking to Lulu, who was currently back home. Kyle Rafferty had agreed to go check on her for us.

"We had a dog, but Trina took him when she left," Ivy had said.

"Can we get a dog?" Dove asked.

"Not right now. Lulu doesn't like dogs."

"Aw, Lulu, do you not like doggies?" Ivy cooed to the fat cat. Lulu just cuddled up in the little girl's lap and fell asleep.

Applause started around us, waking me from my memory.

"Oh, it's starting. Here they come." Vee giggled on the other side of Dove. She looked over at me with a huge smile.

One by one the finalists were introduced and walked to their assigned stations. When they got to Shayla, our row exploded. Dove covered her ears, while Ivy yelled to her big sister.

From the stage, Shayla grinned and gave a little wave.

"Welcome to the final round in the dessert category of the 41st Annual Culinary Arts High School competition!" The announcer paused as the crowd cheered. "As in the other rounds, each contestant will have two hours to create their signature dessert. One they feel matches our theme Old Hollywood Glam! Are our contestants ready?"

They each cheered. Shayla gave a quick look at us in the crowd. We all pumped our fists, clapped, and whooped for her.

"Okay, timer ready ... and goooo!!"

Mr. Duncan Jones and Mrs. Beverly Jones slid into the seats next to Sawyer. I looked over with a smile. Mr. Jones gave a thumbs up. They had traveled here separately to support the kids. Shayla was the only one from Dashwood to make it to the final round. The other five had been eliminated in the earlier rounds.

We watched as the future chefs mixed dough or batter, made ganache or whipped cream. Shayla was calm, moving almost effortlessly through the station. She checked her eclair shells, seemed happy as she pulled them out and put them straight into the chiller.

"I have to go to the bathroom," Ivy said, bouncing in her seat.

"Me too."

I looked at them then at the stage and then at them again. I didn't want to miss anything, but I'm sure it wasn't easy for them to sit this long.

"Alrighty, let's go."

I held their hands as we made our way from our seats to the bathrooms. It was a new experience for all of us, or maybe just me. They took what seemed like forever to go, then I made sure they washed their hands thoroughly.

"Can we get a drink?"

"And some popcorn?"

I wanted to get back to watch Shayla, but I had to remind myself, again, that it must be hard for little kids.

"Yes, whatever you want."

"Yay!" They ran ahead to get in line at the concession stand, pointing at all the different drinks and snacks. They wanted everything.

"You can each get a drink and one snack. We are going to have a nice dinner later."

"After Shayla wins?" Ivy asked.

"Yes, after she wins." I mentally crossed my fingers. I really hoped she did. This competition completely changed my life not that long ago.

With drinks and snacks in hand, we made our way back to our seats. I saw that Shayla was adding the filling to her éclairs now, taking care to fill them fully and evenly.

The girls were good for the next hour and when the buzzer sounded, they cheered.

"It's done," Ivy said. "Can we go now?"

"Did Shayla win?" Dove asked.

"Not yet. They still have to judge," I whispered to them. "But almost."

Finally, the time came to announce the winner. They called fourth and third place first, then had the two finalists step forward.

"And the winner of this year's competition with their creative flavors, cleanliness of workstation and professionalism is ... Shayla Tanner from J.W. Dashwood Fine Arts High School in Dashwood, Texas."

Our whole group jumped to our feet cheering and shouting. Her fellow competitors congratulated her. The chairperson of the competition stepped forward with a large check with her name on it.

She looked straight at me while she accepted the check and I took pictures. Tears of pride ran down my face.

Never in my life did I expect to be in a position like this. Three girls in my care. Granted one was now considered an adult. I loved these girls so much, so quickly.

Later, I sent Rafferty a message to tell him about the day and let him know that Shayla had won. He didn't answer, which was strange. I shrugged it off that he must be busy.

It wasn't until I was climbing into bed, exhausted from the day and full of our yummy celebration dinner, that I got a text from him.

R: **Sorry for the delay. Busy day**

Me: **That's okay. Just wanted to check in.**

R: **I probably shouldn't tell you, but Samir was killed earlier**

Me: **The owner of the Spicy Fig Bistro? Oh no, how?**

R: **Yeah, it's awful. I can fill you in later.**

Me: **Okay.**

I had no idea what to say. Spicy Fig was one of my favorite restaurants and though I'd only met Samir a few times, he had always seemed so nice and friendly. He was always smiling and greeting customers.

R: **Have fun tomorrow. See you soon.**

Me: **See you soon.**

All I could think was how this crime fighting chef thing was nowhere near over. If his death was a murder, I already knew I was all in to help solve it.

The End

Before you go: If you loved Éclairs and Executions, be sure to visit my website to sign up for my newsletter (if you haven't already) and to stay up to date on new releases and other bookish things. When signing up, you will receive **Chef Jessica's Alphabet Soup Recipe** as a free gift. I have "had" it, it is yummy. (Okay, so obviously, it is my recipe, but still, I recommend it!) Continue to the next section for this book's recipe!

Also, check out my other books! You can find links on my website.

www.ejwheltonwrites.com

Recipe:

When I first came up with the name for this book, I was intimidated by the thought of making eclairs. What had I done to myself?

However, it was surprisingly easy but gives the illusion of something fancy or difficult, like you spent all day creating this tasty treat. Don't tell anyone how easy these actually are!

If you've never made them, and give them a try, send me an email about it! I'd love to hear how it goes (ejwheltonwrites@gmail.com)

Choux (the pastry shell):

Ingredients:

½ cup water
½ cup milk
½ cup butter
¼ teaspoon salt
1 teaspoon sugar
1 cup flour
4 to 5 eggs (large or XL eggs do only 4. If using smaller eggs, use 5)

1. In a large saucepan bring to a boil water, milk, butter, salt, and sugar.
2. Once it is boiling add flour, stirring vigorously for 1-2 minutes (I normally do closer to 2 minutes) The dough will firm up almost like Play-Doh consistency.
3. Remove from heat. Let it cool to about 125-135 degrees. You can touch it, but it's still hot. Not burning. (I usually put it in my stand mixer and beat it on low for a minute to release the heat)
4. Add one egg at a time, incorporating completely before adding the next egg. Mixture will be a soft dough/paste but will hold its shape. (I mixed in a stand mixer)
5. Using a plastic piping coupler or piping tip of your choice (but you'll do best with a large opening) and you'll need either a Ziploc bag or piping bag, pipe to desired size. I made about 3-inch long eclairs so I did lines about that size on my parchment.
6. Bake at 425 degrees for 15 minutes then reduce heat to 375 for 12 minutes. Check doneness. Shells should be golden brown and

hollow. (adjust time depending on size. These are for 3- to 4-inch eclairs. Smaller or larger ones will need less or more cooking time)

7. Transfer to a cooling rack to cool completely.

Filling:

You can make any kind of filling you'd like. I am giving a base filling and my personal favorite one is cheesecake pudding.

Ingredients:

1 (3.4 oz) pudding mix (any flavor works)
1 2/3 cup cold milk (2% or whole)
1 tub (8 oz) premade whipped cream (you can also make your own)

1. Whisk cream cheese pudding mix with the milk for about 2-3 minutes. Then mix in whipped cream.
2. Set in the fridge until ready to use.
3. Using a piping bag or Ziploc bag fitted with a small-ish round piping tip, carefully insert into cooled shells. Fill slowly until each is full. If your tip doesn't fill it completely from one side, you can fill from both.

Ganache:

You can use any flavored chips/melting bars. The process is the same.

Ingredients:

1/2 cup chocolate chips
1 tablespoon of vegetable oil (or you can use ¼ cup heavy whipping cream)

1. In microwave-safe bowl, melt chips for 30 seconds at a time, stirring in between until melted. (roughly 30 seconds to a minute should do it).
2. Add half of the oil, stir. Add a little more if the chocolate isn't smooth. Chocolate should become smooth and glossy.
3. Dip or drizzle chocolate over the top of eclairs. Let ganache cool and set.
4. Enjoy!
5. Store in fridge.

Author note:

Thank you once again for reading one of my stories. This one was a hard fought battle to get into print. It just wouldn't come out of my head onto the paper (well, computer). Once I broke it loose, the characters took over and fought with me until the bitter end.

The end? That was all their idea. I had a different idea in mind, but no, oh, no, they yelled and screamed and threw themselves on the floor, refusing to talk to me until I did what they said.

I also want to talk about found family. Even if you have a wonderful family, you can find family in your friends. You know what I mean? Those friends who are more than just a buddy, a pal, but you count them as a second mom, dad or a sister, brother, uncle... whatever!

Being in the military years ago, I had that found family. Can't make it home for the holidays? Not to worry, we aren't going home either, let's get together.

When I had my first child, I had so much love and support. Plus, so many gobs of hand-me-downs that she could wear a different outfit every single day and not wear them all.

If you have a "found family," you know how important they are.

Well, see you for Falafels and Fatalities. It is very (and I mean very) loosely based on a local restaurant and the family who owned it. I hope you'll consider pre-ordering it, so you don't miss out!

Until the next book, happy reading.

www.ejwheltonwrites.com